The Oath and Blood Price

Part One

Rise of The Mercenary King Saga Book One

By Peter-Shaun Tyrell

For Aminata, without whom this book would still be just an idea

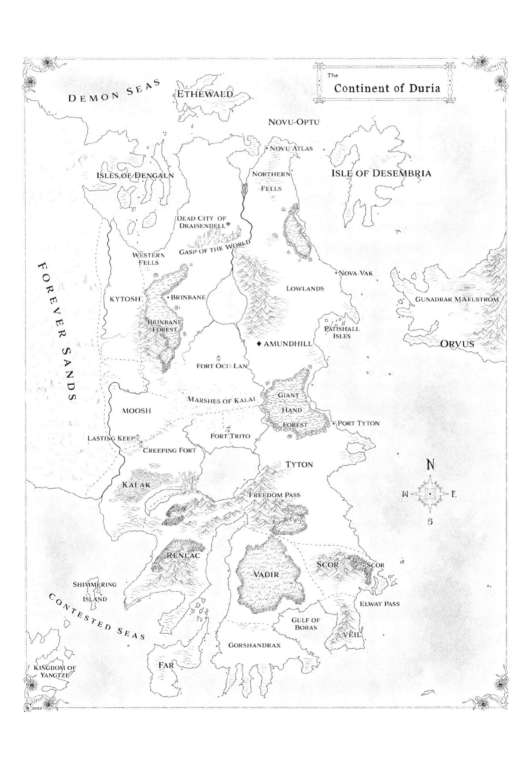

Chapter One

The night air was cool. Thalkin let out his breath as the trees rustled in the breeze. When the gust died down, he sucked in a lungful of air and held it. The footsteps were getting closer, the voices clearer. It was Gregori and his two lackeys. They were arguing about who was better at skimming stones with Jon and Dill confessing that Gregori was probably the best. Thalkin snarled at their arse-kissing. Even as his arms struggled to keep his position high up in the tree, with a sack full of pears on his back, he couldn't help but hate the way that his companions licked the boots of their leader.

Give me a stone and we'll see who's best at skimming Thalkin thought.

His arms began to shake, and he struggled to keep silent, letting out small breaths. If they found Thalkin on Boldon Thomil's farm they would certainly give him a beating. He could see their forms in the darkness walk past the tree below. They were passing something between them and bringing it to their lips. Just a few more steps. Another gust of wind gently blew through Farmer Thomil's land, and the rustling of the thousands of leaves gave Thalkin some respite as he repositioned himself quickly, shaking off the strain he felt in his arms as he continued to perch in the tree. By the time the wind had died down, Gregori and his friends had walked past and Thalkin let out a sigh of relief.

As he made to move down the tree, he heard a tear, followed by a ripping and a cascade of bumps and bangs. His eyes grew wide with terror as he realised what was happening. The entire contents of his sack came tumbling down, hitting every branch, making enough sound to warrant the suspicion of the three boys.

'Who's there?' Gregori sounded scared for a moment, which made Thalkin grin. 'Come down at once, or I shall fetch my father.'

'Gregori, let us go. It was just the wind.' The squeaking voice of Dill crept up cracking with fear.

'This is my father's land, Dill. I shall know who sneaks about in it.'

Thalkin thought it was useless hiding now. He started his descent down from the large pear tree. Its golden leaves sat upon a 30-foot tree, nothing too hard for Thalkin but apparently, they put the other pear trees in Duria to shame. The whole continent knew about the perry that was made in this land, thanks to the sugar stalks and the golden pear trees that Scor was famous for all over Duria. The small town had grown as its economy thrived off Thomil's farm. And Thalkin was stealing from it. He dropped down and began to nonchalantly pick the pears up and put them back into his half-torn sack.

'Well, well, well, if it isn't our very own Orphan of Scor. Welcome to my father's farm once again, Thalkin. Would you like Jon to help you carry your stolen goods?' mocked Gregori. The son of Lord Thomil, Gregori was a tall, sinewy boy. He had bright blond hair that he tucked behind his ears. His eyes were brown, with long lashes and high cheekbones, and his whole face was soft with straight lines and perfect curves. Thalkin hated it.

'Past your bedtime, isn't it Gregori? Doesn't papa know you've taken one of the perry bottles out to play with? Or do your little friends need some coaxing before you give them a little kiss later tonight?' Thalkin suggested.

Gregori's face went dark, but then turned into a sneer, which showed his pristine white teeth 'Kissing? Maybe I can bring your mother to teach us? Oh, sorry I forgot, she's dead.'

Thalkin ground his teeth. Anger coursed through him and he felt a deep rage building inside. His mind froze and he could not think of a reply.

'Let's smash his teeth in, Gregori. That whoreson bastard hasn't had a beating in a while,' Jon said, cracking his large knuckles.

'No, he hasn't, has he?' Gregori looked very thoughtful. 'It has been several months since we broke his face and those little orphan ribs.' They all laughed and Thalkin ground his teeth, as the memory of that night rose to the surface. The front of Thalkin's shoulder-length, jet-black hair was tied behind his head with everything behind his ears flowing freely. He normally wore his hair down, not caring much about his looks, but this style stopped it from blocking his vision. It just so happened that it would also help him in a fight.

He swallowed his anger. After that brutal beating he had been taking lessons on how to contain himself. He did not know his mother, so she meant nothing to him. 'Listen Gregori, you weren't supposed to take the perry and I wasn't meant to take the pears. Let us both be on our way and---'

'Filthy urchin! You dare speak to me like that, suggesting such a thing. I thought we taught you a lesson but obviously we failed. Stealing from my father? You are lucky I won't tell him. Jon remind this rodent of his lesson.'

Jon snarled and stomped over menacingly. His huge shoulders leading his march forward, his tree trunk legs almost shaking the ground beneath him. Having lived just sixteen summers, Jon was the same size as most men in the town. Thalkin, being an orphan, was scrawny, lean and small. He had spent months hiding away from the town ever since that dark night. Yet he wasn't idle. He had found someone to teach him some new skills. Ones that he was about to put into practice.

Thalkin pulled up his fists and began to bob up and down on his toes. Jon paid this no mind and charged wildly at him. Thalkin easily dodged the barreling man child and pressed his body up against Jon's. He pinned him against a nearby tree and began hammering punches just to the side of Jon's spine. His kidneys.

Jon raged and swung a clumsy downward strike. Thalkin side-stepped and swung a right hook which caught the big man in his body again. Jon stumbled, more from his missed punch than anything else. Thalkin wasn't trying to punch Jon's face yet, he had to work the body first. Just as he'd been told. It might not look like much, but Jon's body was already starting to feel the effects, just the large boy didn't realise it yet. He lunged at Thalkin again trying to grab him. Thalkin tried to duck again but Jon was quicker this time. He had a handful of Thalkin's shirt and threw a quick jab, ringing Thalkin's ear. Fortunately, Thalkin was moving out the way so he didn't take the full brunt of the blow, yet it still stung like a thousand bees. Thalkin knew how to escape though; he twisted away from Jon's grip, forcing his arm to bend unnaturally and thus let go. He was now slightly off-balance which let Thalkin throw a big right into his kidney. He stumbled from the punch now and a look of pain was evident on his face. Jon's guard dropped down to his sides and that's when Thalkin switched it up. He moved inside and threw a few well-placed jabs into Jon's face, clipping his jaw several times. It forced his guard up and Thalkin dropped his aim to the body, the guard came down and Thalkin worked his head. Jon started to howl with pain and rage. Any focus or concentration deserted the oaf who now started to swing wildly, breathing heavily. Thalkin backed off, his movements small and efficient, just waiting for an opening. It didn't take long as the fatigue from the wild swings and punches to the body became too much for Jon who now stood there with his arms at his side. Thalkin was on him in an instant, he pulled his fist back behind his body, bent his knees and crashed a vicious uppercut under Jon's chin. He fell backwards with deadweight like a tree that had been felled, unmoving.

Smiling, Thalkin turned to pick up his sack but something tackled him hard around the waist and he fell face-first into the ground. He scrambled up but punches and kicks followed him as he made to rise. Dill and Gregori had launched an assault on Thalkin. He regained his bearing and began to duck, dive, and dodge the oncoming attacks. He had to save his energy and let the other two tire, and judging from Dill's body, he would be the first. Gregori had pulled away slightly and Dill threw a lazy punch at Thalkin. Dill was a squat boy with arms too small for his body, so it was easy for Thalkin to dodge. Dill was sent crashing to the ground as Thalkin ducked and move inside his guard and sent a whipping hooked punch to his puffy cheek. Moving with the momentum, Thalkin then barged into Gregori and they both toppled over. Gregori was quick on his feet and began to throw punches, one landed sharply on Thalkin's already crooked nose and he backed away, eyes watering. Gregori took this opportunity and grabbed Thalkin by the waist again, lifting him off his feet. Gregori was throwing wild punches but most of them were hitting Thalkin's guard. His forearms were hurting but at least his face was not. For a moment Gregori's barrage stopped and Thalkin could hear his ragged breath. He reached up and in a split-second was bringing Gregori's face to his as he brought his forehead up. With a crack like a skull breaking, Thalkin's head collided with Gregori's nose.

Gregori rolled off moaning in pain as blood oozed from the broken nose. With weary legs Thalkin stood, leaning on a tree for support. The victor of the brawl laughed tiredly and surveyed the scene around him. It was much different to the one several months ago, when all three boys had stood over him, laughing at his broken body. He picked up his sack of pears and made his way off Thomil's farm.

The young orphan made it out of the farm without further incident and moved constantly, varying his pace between a jog and a walk. His red face and ragged breath would make him a target for the town guard, but then again being the town's chief urchin made him a target, so making himself as least noticeable as possible was important. He needed to get to Edgir's home before midnight otherwise the drunken fool would most likely be too deep in his tankard to open the door, so a balance of speed and unassuming nonchalance was needed. He reached the town of Scor proper as the outskirts that made the border were left behind. The town was showing signs of growth everywhere. The sky was clear, and a cooling breeze gently washed over Thalkin as he made his way through the skeletons of the various new buildings. Warehouses, homes, taverns and temples were rising like a stone forest around him. Even at this late hour, some buildings were still being worked on by the dim lights of a lantern, identified by the sound of a single hammer clanging down or the burning of a furnace as sand and potash were melted together.

The inns and taverns were always full as the town provided a steady flow of work from all corners of Duria, but Thalkin steered clear of them as the town guard were in short supply and so focused instead on the most troublesome areas. He knew the streets, they were his veins that channelled themselves around the body of Scor, and he knew their every hidden nook and shadowy cranny. He was making good time when he came upon a trader struggling with his pony that was hauling the wagon containing his goods. The man's ebony skin glistened with sweat as he vainly tried to pull on the pony's reigns. He was lean with sharp features and the traditional robes of the people of Kytosh, which were dusty and well-travelled. His head scarf was coming loose upon his head making him look extremely exasperated.

'Come on you beast!' he snarled as he pulled, his boots slipping in the mud.

Thalkin leant on the wall and watched for a few moments before the trader turned to him.

'Would you rather watch boy, or give me assistance?' His voice was thick with the Northern accent.

Thalkin smiled. He walked over and carefully placed the torn sack on the back of the wagon and began to pull. Thalkin's skinny frame did little to help and the two were worn out after a few moments. 'What's wrong with the beast?' Thalkin puffed.

'He's hungry. I sold everything I had and stocked up for the journey to Scor with these wares.' He walked around to the side of the wagon and tapped it, then pulled out a water skin and took a mouthful. He handed it to Thalkin. At first, Thalkin didn't register it; no one offered him anything unless he was under their bind. 'Well, you thirsty boy?'

Thalkin took the skin and took a much-needed drink. He tried his best not to take too many a mouthful as this man was clearly in as bad a position as him, maybe even worse. An orphan of the South was always cared for, it was a tradition that they would never go without food or shelter. The orphans were entrusted to their Binds which changed every month. Every household would have a responsibility towards the orphans or the uncared for. In Scor, however, things were much different. The town was on the verge of becoming one of the independent states of Boras, splitting from Tyton so that it could govern itself. It needed rapid growth before it became truly independent so little time was given to orphans. Tradition still dictated that he would be fed and sheltered though it was kept at a minimum. Thalkin had spent many a nights with a growling stomach and chattering teeth. It was not uncommon for Thalkin to skip his Binds as he would fare worse in their household than on the street.

He nodded his thanks and handed back the water skin. 'Where are you headed?'

'The Flayed Dragon Inn.'

'Of course. A good Inn. Maybe costly for a man in your situation.'

He drew himself up, obviously taking offence. 'My situation is none of your concern.' he said. The man had a square face, with bright blue eyes that made quite a contrast to his skin. His lips were cracked from the travel no doubt and Thalkin could see no hair on his head or a hairline that went beyond his head-scarf. He wasn't fat but Thalkin could tell this man liked the comforts of food and wine.

Thalkin shrugged off the comment and placed his hand in the sack. He took three pears and walked in front of the pony. He presented a hand in front of the pony's face and it reached out for the pear. Thalkin took a step back and the pony took a step forward. Thalkin repeated this and began leading the horse down the road. Thalkin sensed the beast knew what was happening and stopped, so he held his hand out flat with the pear and the pony greedily chomped it up, juices squirting from its mouth. Thalkin giggled.

'Thank you, young sir,' the trader said, with relief in his voice. Thalkin held out the pears and the man took them. Repeating what Thalkin had done, he took a small bite from one of the pears and led the pony onwards.

'My journey is farther along from the Flayed Dragon. I hope you don't mind if I walk along till then?'

'Fine by me.'

They both walked in silence as the pony strained to reach the pears. The creaking of the wagon under the great strain of the goods in the back was the only noise that broke the silence. Although the town was growing most of the roads were muddened but fortunately for the trader, it had not rained during the past few nights, so the ground was not wet. Thalkin could feel him being looked at and sensed a question was going to be directed at him. 'What is the news of Scor then?' the trader asked eventually. From the man's tone, Thalkin knew he was desperately trying to start a conversation. It must have been a lonely journey with just a stubborn pony for company.

'There is nothing I can tell you that you have not heard which brought you down here,' Thalkin shrugged.

'That I do not believe,' the tired-looking traveller said, inclining his head towards Thalkin, pressing the question.

'Well, Farmer Boldon Thomil is basically the Lord Procterate in all but name, he owns anything worth of note and the town owes its rise thanks to him.'

'Of course.'

'We have many travellers coming through. New faces are common, so the town guard are always on edge so be careful with that. The town's residents are welcoming to newcomers but keep a close eye on them until they prove their loyalty.'

'Unusual for some towns.'

Thalkin nodded. 'Thomil proposed that the town needs to grow, in every way. including its population. Workers, traders, craftsmen, even fighters.'

'Is the towns guard you refer to thin in numbers?'

'Aye. After a hard day's work people tend to gravitate towards the inns to try the world-famous perry and rum this town offers. This in turn, leads to brawls; nothing serious but too much slows down progress.' Thalkin's voice began to grow bitter.

It wasn't missed by the trader and they both lapsed back into silence until they neared the corner, when Thalkin's new companion couldn't help but continue some conversation. 'Do you have a beast yourself?'

Thalkin barked a laugh with little humour. 'I own only what is on my back. If you make any money, I would suggest selling the pony in exchange for a shire horse. Did you bring this all the way from Kytosh?'

The trader shook his head 'I bought him in Renlac after traveling down the Spine of Duria on a river boat. I had to sell my previous horse for the journey down the river.'

Thalkin knew with his minimal understanding that even a journey for a pony from Renlac may have been a bit too much, especially if the trader was as under-provisioned as he said he was. 'You must have something truly special under the wagon.'

'Oh, I do indeed. Not only did I spend every last piece of copper, but I called in every favour to acquire this potential fortune.' He grinned, flashing his yellowing teeth. The man really did need some provisions, his mouth looked like it wasn't too far from becoming diseased. Thalkin knew all about what a lack of fruit and nourishment could do to a man. 'Maybe you will be able to spare a few coins for what I have?'

Thalkin smiled sadly and instead of responding said 'You will carry on down the street and skip the next two left turns. After which there will be a street that opens up into a square, the Flayed Dragon Inn is there. It is Scor's main square.' Thalkin took his sack and began to walk away.

'I am Momo, young friend, and you?' He beamed a smile at Thalkin. The wagon creaking as it went; the pony snorting its tiredness and annoyance at Momo.

Thalkin turned with a grim face. 'My name is Thalkin, the Orphan of Scor, Momo. And some friendly advice, if you want any success in Scor, I would advise against naming me your friend.' He nodded his goodbye and continued onwards to Edgir's home.

Edgir had once been a rival of Boldon Thomil's, Gregori's Father. For centuries, the village of Scor had been a bane for Tyton. Its vulnerability to raids and the distance from the capital of the state meant it was a drain on the largest Borasian State. Boldon Thomil's father began an economic revolution that had made even greater strides thanks to his son. Edgir had owned vast amounts of land which were bought up by the Thomil family and, according to the rumours, had manufactured a trade deal with the remnants of the Elven Kingdom in the Veil to the South. It had brought the Thomil's great riches and Edgir had struggled to keep up, eventually being completely bought out. He had turned to drink to escape his obvious failure on seizing the opportunity that lay with the Elves. The old Masters had sat behind their hills and natural fort to the south for centuries. Driven to near extinction by the freed men and their

Godmen Liberators, they were fearful of any contact with their destructors. Yet several hundred years after the human civil war, known as the Schism, the men of the South who defied the Godmen reached out to their former slavers and offered them free and safe movement among the Borasian States. This freedom had not been truly taken up by the elves as it was rare to see them beyond their borders, but trade did happen. Elven goods had become more accessible and soon people wanted their wares, trinkets and weapons, as well as the other way round. Scor provided an important trade hub and route for both men and elves. Even the dwarven kingdoms over the Contested Seas were now accessible being old allies of the elves. Dwarves were not as rare than elves in the North, though still not common.

Suffice to say Edgir was a shadow of his former self. He had been kicked out of every tavern and inn in the town, even the ones he used to own. He was not devoid of his senses however and still remembered how to brew his own mead and wine. He thus enlisted Thalkin to steal the necessary ingredients to make his own ale, bonus rewards were given if it was off Thomil's farm. In exchange, Edgir was to part his knowledge over to Thalkin. Being a street urchin of Scor, Thalkin knew that he would either die in the streets or become something. Only learning and understanding how the world worked would help him to do this and as no one would give this freely he would have to barter for it. In exchange for his services, Thalkin asked for lessons, lessons in anything. He had learned how to gut and cook a fish from a local fish monger in exchange for catching fish for her in the nearby lake. This, of course, was stopped when he was discovered fishing on Thomil's Lake, but the skill he had learnt was worth the severe beating. He had learnt his letters by helping the local scholar sneak notes to a tavern owner's wife. He did not get caught on that deal. A local trader taught him the dialects of the other Borasian states, but only after Thalkin had given him details about some the town people's vices, vital information which helped him to target what his customers wanted.

Edgir however was teaching him how to fight. Dengaln Fist, or Den Fist as Edgir called it was a fighting style that had been adopted by the men of Dengaln. Most men of Duria fought using the art of Pugilism; it was only in the land of Far and the Freelands that different fighting styles were seen. Most men knew how to brawl, but Edgir was a master of the Den Fist. In his youth, he had travelled the world seeking the most skilled exponents of fighting. Edgir had claimed he had bested every single one of them in one of his drunken speeches outside of a tavern one night. Most people laughed as he was an old, drunken failure but Thalkin had believed him. He had helped him home and Edgir promised to teach him the art of Den Fist in exchange for helping him to get mead, ale or anything that could help his drunken state be maintained and his lesson would continue tonight.

As he turned the corner of Edgir's lonely street, the last vestige of his empire was a set of drooping dilapidated cottages. Most of the houses were unoccupied, so Edgir's was the only one with lights in the window. Thalkin came to a stop outside and he felt the exhaustion catch up with him as he looked up at the Summer Moon. He knocked lazily on the door and heard something being knocked over as someone made their way to the door.

'Who is it?' a raspy, broken voice demanded from the other side of the door.

Thalkin sighed. 'It's me.'

'Thalkin?'

'Open up, Edgir I'm tired.'

The door creaked open and Edgir's face peered through the gap. The once straight-backed, authoritative, bear of a man, was now a skulking mess. All his hair had almost fallen out, his skin was yellowed and cracked veins spread about his face like vines wrapping themselves around an old oak tree. 'Well, don't just stand there you're letting out all the cold.' He moved aside and Thalkin pushed his way through. The place was in the same mess as usual. The door led to a fairly large room, enough for a table with several chairs around. All of them had either wineskins, or clothes thrown over them. There was a cabinet standing on one side with its doors wide open; inside were various tools for making one's own ale. The kitchen was on the far side of the room. It looked like it had not seen a duster or a wet cloth in years. Dishes were piled high and a small number of flies danced around it. There were two doors on Thalkin's left, the closest was the bathroom. This had a fairly large tub inside, but Thalkin knew it was not an instrument to clean but to ferment ale instead, and any other beverage that was needed to quench Edgir's thirst. The other room was Edgir's bedroom which had always remained shut when Thalkin was there. There was a cushioned chair next to the window on the far right, the only thing that was not used as a shelf in the whole room, which was, of course, Edgir's drink chair. It was there for him to stare out and ponder how his life had stooped so low.

Thalkin dropped the sack of pears on the table. 'I'll need a new sack if you plan on sending me back there.'

Edgir studied it and huffed. 'I can stitch it.'

'With those shaking hands?' Thalkin laughed.

Edgir snarled at him. 'Watch your mouth boy.'

Thalkin looked away. Even as drunk as he constantly was, Edgir could still fight and lay Thalkin unconscious with the flick of an elbow if he wanted to.

Edgir let it go and turned to the pears. He cradled the ripped sack in his arms and carried them into the bathroom, dropping them into the bath, the tumbling sounds of a new batch of Edgir's Perry, soon to be made. Before long, he came back into the room, saying: 'You've brought me a few over the last few days I should be set for a while now.'

'That's right, and you promised me a final lesson.'

Edgir nodded and suddenly lashed out with a front kick into Thalkin's stomach. It took the boy by surprise and he landed on his rump. Edgir stepped forward in the Den Fist stance but Thalkin kicked out and rolled up. They both squared up and Edgir smiled, a sparkle in his eye. They exchanged blows back and forth. Few punches landed and the ones that did were rolled off the shoulders. Kicks lashed out at thighs, some were blocked, but most slapped the muscle. The room had sufficient space, but chairs and tankards were still sent flying across the room as the two sparred. Edgir's weathered and trained muscles took the blows as they came, while Thalkin did his best, but his legs began to fatigue. He was losing so he feigned a slow punch. Edgir swiped hard with his back leg, but Thalkin raised his knee to deflect the kick. He came down hard with his foot and channelled the momentum forward in an elbow strike that lashed

13

down. The blow didn't land but Edgir faltered and Thalkin charged forward throwing a barrage of punches. Some started to land as Edgir's guard began to tire. Just as Thalkin was getting the upper hand, Edgir turned his back. Thalkin then dropped his guard and aimed to finish the assault by choking his opponent from behind. It didn't go quite to plan as Edgir came back around with the back of his fist hitting Thalkin square in the jaw. As the ground came to meet Thalkin and his vision dimmed he caught sight of Edgir's face, the eyes manic while the bloody lips cracked into a mad grin.

Thalkin woke with the pain throbbing at his jaw. Something wet and cold slapped against his face and Thalkin went to push it off, but there was strong resistance.

'Sorry about that. Got a little carried away, but then again so did you.' Edgir pressed the cold slab of meat into Thalkin's face.

'I've got it, Edgir.' Thalkin said in a muffled voice. He could smell some of the salt that helped to preserve the meat and realized just how hungry he was.

He moved his hand away and walked into the bathroom, where Edgir had already begun his process of fermentation. Thalkin tried to stand but his head began to spin so he resigned himself to staying on the floor for the moment.

'What did you hit me with?'

Edgir's face popped around the door. 'It's called dead weight. The human body is a strange thing, you can ball your fist up or tense your muscles as much as you want but if you can just harness your weight into a weapon it can do far more damage. A back-spinning punch is a solid way to achieve this. It is nothing but bone and the weight of all your muscle, blood and fat crashing into someone.' He walked over and offered his hand out to Thalkin, who took it and stood up. He began demonstrating the move he did. 'It is best used when the person coming at you thinks they have the advantage, so they drop their guard completely, like you did. You won't catch me with it, I'm too smart but try it on your tormentors if you see them again.'

'I will.' Thalkin left out the story of his fight. The story of him being caught by Gregori might not be the best way to advertise his services.

'Well you've learned your lesson, I think it is time you should be off.'

'But Edgir it is far from dawn, Sal and Rosalind will not be up this at time.' Sal and Rosalind were the family he was currently bound too. They lived some distance away in one of the newer areas of Scor.

Edgir shrugged his shoulders and went back to his bathroom. 'If I need you again, I shall send word somehow.'

Thalkin was left alone in the living room. He found some hard bread on the table and shoved it into his pocket and walked out, slamming the door behind him with the meat still pressed against his sore jaw. The moon hung high in the sky, awaiting the Father Sun to rise. It was a few hours before dawn, which was when Sal would wake up and head out for work. Thalkin had a few places to sleep outside. He was lucky it was still summer, so the nights were not too bad. He still clutched his cloak around him though, the night air was still not the same as a house with a hearth. He made his way over to the side of town where Sal and Rosalind lived. He would aim for a few hours' sleep until the sun would wake him and then he hoped to sneak into the house before Rosalind came into his room to wake him. He felt bad about interrupting Sal's sleep before his work, so he had to aim for a small window between Sal leaving for work and Rosalind waking him up. He walked past one of the new buildings that was in the process of being built which he had squatted in before. A merchant who had come into money was adding his contribution to the growth of the town by opening a tavern that specialized in the cuisine from Far. The building had not been completed yet and the merchant was staying in the Flayed Dragon until it was finished.

Thalkin made his way around and looked for an opening. The windows and doors were boarded-up for now so there was no direct way in but Thalkin knew of a way. He scaled the timber logs that made up the walls of the building and trod carefully along the roof. The town was quiet now, as its inhabitants were all asleep, apart from the night shift of the guard that patrolled the streets. There was little chance of Thalkin being caught as the meagre number of town guard could barely keep up their normal patrols at this time. However, there was always a chance of this so Thalkin quickly got to the chimney and found that, just like the previous nights the hearth had not been boarded-up. He shimmied down and dropped when he was a few feet from the bottom. As dark as it was outside there was no moonlight inside the inn, so it was pitch black. Thalkin had already stayed here and knew the layout somewhat. Near the entrance there was a cluster of cushioned chairs. The wooden floor and walls had no furs up so the air was cold inside. He pushed a few chairs together to make a makeshift bed and made himself as comfortable as possible. He pulled out some bread and meat that he stole from Edgir and wolfed it down. His jaw hurt as he chewed but he was too hungry to care. His knuckles were bruised from the fight with Gregori and Edgir. He counted his injuries and took them all as lessons. He would never blindly charge at an opponent again, especially if he knew the opponent had tricks up their sleeves. As much as Thalkin now knew there was always someone who knew more. He finished off his food as he thought about this and pulled his cloak around him. Sleep was not hard for him to find and he was soon falling into a deep slumber.

Chapter Two

Thalkin woke up feeling damp and shivering with the new day's light piercing through a crack in the boarded-up windows and shining in his face. He roused himself and made for the chimney. He shimmied himself up and was out in a few minutes. Luckily, it had never been lit, so he only had debris from the stone masonry on his clothes, rather than soot. He dropped down from the roof quickly, making sure he wasn't seen, then straightened himself up, wrapped his cloak around him and made for Sal's and Rosalind's home. The Black Moon was high, pulling the Father Sun up behind it. The early morning sun gave the sky an orange cloak that rolled over the bottom of the clouds. The Black Moon started to rise before the sun, but it only became visible when the light breached the horizon. It would disappear around dusk, always clearing the path for the sun to follow. Many tales were told about the Black Moon, how it was the sun's older brother, that had burnt out from creating the world, and when this sun burnt out, one of the white moons of the night would take its place. Other tales spoke of how it was a demon that the sun chased away. Thalkin used to like that one. He stopped gazing toward the heavens and started his journey. Most likely he would have missed Sal. It would not matter much but Thalkin preferred not to face any trouble. Most of the families that he was bound too would take their anger or annoyance out on him so had learned not to give them any excuses to do so. Being found on the street by the town guard would generally bring shame to the family. Some did not care, but others thought a lot of their honour. He had already missed his first night with his current family so he could not miss another one. Thalkin was only a few streets away now but he still wanted to get there quickly. Hopefully, he would just miss Sal but get there in time to sneak into bed before being roused by Rosalind. He turned sharply onto the street the couple lived on and was knocked over by something unmovable. He fell on his backside and scraped his palm on the floor. Looking up he saw a large stoic man standing over him.

'Are you OK, Thalkin?' Sal asked kindly, his hand extending out to him.

Thalkin took the large hand and felt the calluses upon the mason's hand. 'Yes, I'll be fine.'

Sal was as broad as they come. He had a shaven head, like most masons and a face that had aged from days of working out in the open sky. In most of the conversations that Thalkin had had with him, Sal was almost impossible to read. He spoke little and reacted as much as the stone he worked with to anything that was said.

'You were out all night.' He was stating a fact.

'Yes. I didn't want to wake you when I realised it was so late.'

Sal nodded but Thalkin saw his eyes glide over the bruises on his face and hands. 'Not in any trouble?'

'Just being a boy.'

'You are nearly a man now, Thalkin, fifteen years you have now lived.' Sal went to walk away but stopped for a moment 'It is the tradition of the South to look after the bastards but don't bring any trouble to my home.'

Thalkin shrugged.

Before leaving Sal looked away, thinking about something. 'Rosalind has just finished preparing food. Head inside, there should be some left.' With that he marched away.

Thalkin spat on the floor and walked towards the cottage. On both sides of the street new cottages had been built. They all had two floors with thatched rooves, with walls made of brilliant white stone and timber. The houses were quite wide with windows on either side of the entrance and a small garden that sat in front giving some distance between the houses and the side of the road. Thalkin finally came to the cottage he was currently living in and opened the door. The smell of the food hit him straight away, making his stomach churn and cry out in pain. He could smell bacon, sausages, boiled eggs, bread, honey cakes, milk and other delicacies. Sal's stomach seemed to know no end and Rosalind was more than happy to prepare banquets for him. Thalkin had only stayed with the two one previous night but he had never eaten so much in his life. He would have counted himself lucky to be with this family but, generally, something or someone would smash him in the face and ruin it. He ignored these thoughts and tried to enjoy it whilst it lasted. He was standing in the hall of the house that had three doors and stairs leading up. To his right, was his current room, and to his left was a living room where the family could gather by the fire and the kitchen was opposite him. The stairs climbed to his left as he made for the kitchen. Inside, there was a long table that spanned the length of the room. At one end, there was a huge plate that had all the things that Thalkin could smell and more, including berries and fruits, a bowl of oats and that black disc-shaped item that Rosalind claimed was blood sausage. To Thalkin, however, it tasted like pure evil. It was a custom that the couple had brought from their homeland, Renlac and Thalkin believed it should have stayed there. When Thalkin first said this, he regretted it immediately, thinking he would have his head taken off his shoulders by Sal's fist, but Rosalind burst out laughing and Sal smiled. The only time he ever saw him react, come to think of it.

Rosalind herself was at the sink washing some pots and pans. She hadn't noticed Thalkin walk in and was quietly humming a tune to herself, looking out at the garden. Most of the new cottages had been built with a garden and Rosalind had already started to craft it to her design and spent most of her time in it.

'Did Sal not eat today?' Thalkin did not want to believe it was his.

Rosalind jumped, her hand shooting to her chest expecting her heart to burst out. 'Thalkin!' She laughed 'You cannot sneak around like that.'

Thalkin nodded his apologies looking at the food.

'And no, this is yours. You constantly look like you've never eaten. I have lived in this town a few months now and you have looked like you are one meal away from death.'

'You are perceptive then.' Thalkin took a tentative seat, barely controlling himself.

'Thalkin, your face.' Rosalind's hands rose to touch the young boy but stopped and she backed away.

'It's nothing, I promise,' he said trying to reassure her.

Rosalind still looked concerned but she changed the subject back to food. 'Didn't the other families feed you? Surely, Scor upholds the custom?'

'You haven't been in Scor long have you? I am the one and only Orphan of Scor and most wish that I did not exist.' Thalkin's hands crept to his knife and fork. 'They feed me, sometimes but mostly I have to scavenge for myself. It's not too bad, most of the time they are not looking at me because they don't have the time, so I steal if I am really hungry.'

Rosalind looked hurt by this but smiled through it, reassuringly. 'Well, what are you waiting for, break your fast, I have a few jobs for you today.' She turned and began to clean the dishes again, her red-golden hair flashing as sun-beams shone through the garden window. The straight strands of her hair looked almost like sunrays themselves as they caught the light, the odd grey hair drowned out in the sunlight. Thalkin snapped out of his revere and his attention was brought quickly around to the food in front of him and the feast began. Admittedly, it was over quickly.

Thalkin sat back groaning his delight. There was still food left on the plate, but he had managed to eat most of it. Rosalind was getting things ready for her shift in the garden.

'Truly Rosalind, I have never eaten so good. Thank you.'

'Well, I'm glad you enjoyed it.'

Thalkin was feeling tired. He stood up and stretched, making his way towards the second bedroom that had been designated to him whilst he was staying with the couple.

'Excuse me, Thalkin.' He turned to Rosalind's voice raising his eyebrows. 'Where do you think you are going?' she asked, hands on her hips.

'I am going to sleep, I had a rough night and that food has made me tired.'

Rosalind clicked her tongue and said, 'Well that's what you get for making me worry. You are going to help me in the garden, then you are going to take Sal's lunch over to him and bring me back some things from the market. Then I will allow you to sleep.' And she smiled.

Thalkin's mouth dropped open. 'A jest surely, Rosalind?'

Rosalind laughed. 'The next time you think about not coming back, remember this.' She walked over and pushed Thalkin towards the wooden bucket that had all the garden tools in it. Thalkin picked it up and with a resigned sigh made his way out to the garden.

'Rosalind, I have been beaten, whipped, stolen from, yelled at, and this is the worst punishment I have ever received.' Thalkin laughed shaking his head as he set the bucket down beside the loosened soil that would soon be sprouting the range of vegetables, fruit and flowers. He turned to say something to Rosalind, but she was still standing in the doorway, her brown eyes full of concern. She wasn't crying but tears began to form.

'Is it really that bad for you, Thalkin?'

Thalkin was taken aback by the tone in her voice. He shook his head. 'I jest Rosalind, of course I jest. The fine people of Scor are decent upstanding people.' He began to unload the tools as he had seen Rosalind do on his first day. He moved to fill the watering can with water from the pump. 'They adhere to the tradition of the South of looking after the neglected like every great nation of the Borasian States.' The sarcasm was not lost on Rosalind who had moved over to Thalkin. She lay her hand lightly on Thalkin's who stopped the pumping. The anger had been building up inside him as he had talked, and he noticed his knuckles were white and the metal pump handle dug into his palm. He looked at her and she smiled sadly. A silent communication passed between each other and Rosalind took over the pumping. They did not talk about it for the rest of the day.

The two got on with the garden work, however. It was fairly sizeable, designed for both a place of leisure and a place of productivity. Thomil wanted the families to have their own sources of food, to reduce the need for Scor's farms and the ones that stretched up and down Duria. Self-sufficiency would maximise the profits of Scor as it entered this new era.

For some time, the two quietly tended the garden. Thalkin felt relaxation descend on him as his whole world focused on the caring of the plants and vegetables. It was hard but enjoyable work and he could feel the sweat form on his brow as the sun began to increase the heat of the day. Rosalind pumped some water into two pewter cups and Thalkin made short work of his.

'You know, you should put some on the back of your neck as well. It helps cool your body down.'

Rosalind advised.

Thalkin raised his eyebrows with interest. 'Is this true?'

'My father was a hunter in Renlac, he was part of the fur trade that our country is famous for. He was exposed to the sun a lot, and to keep himself cool, he would not only drink water but also take a handful and splash it on his face and neck, which would help stop him from succumbing to the heat.'

Thalkin nodded taking note of this. He asked Rosalind to continue talking about her homeland, so they talked awhile and Thalkin learned about her country. He took every word in because, more than anything he knew that knowledge would be what helped him to escape his urchin life. It would just be about applying that knowledge in the necessary direction. They continued working on, talking about various things and topics. Thalkin finally stood up and groaned at the aching pain in his young muscles. The groan turned into a long yawn.

Rosalind looked at the work that he'd completed and sighed 'Ok, that's enough for today, you can go.'

Thalkin bowed his thanks. 'Thank you, this has worked me hard. The sleep will be welcomed.' He heard a scoff behind him and winced.

'Sleep? No, I mean you can go and do the rest of the jobs I have asked you to do. Then you can come home and have something to eat, then you have my permission to sleep.'

Thalkin almost collapsed. 'Rosalind, please.'

'Thalkin, in Scor, people may not care for their duty, but in Renlac we take the life of the orphaned child seriously. Do you know where the tradition came from?'

Thalkin's brow furrowed, he had never thought about it and shook his head.

'Long ago, before the Godmen freed mankind from the shackles of the elves, we were slaves to their whim. You know this history?'

Thalkin nodded. Everyone who had a hearth for people to gather around to tell such stories knew of Uthanarax's Gift, the first of the Godmen who bestowed knowledge on the simple-minded man.

'Our ancestors could barely look after themselves whilst under the elvish whip. Mothers found it difficult to look after more than one child. They had to choose which child to look after, Thalkin. Basically, our ancestors chose which child would most likely die. Life improved for our people after the Godmen freed us, but it was still difficult. The Godmen, even though they raised our ancestors from the mud, were too great to understand the loss of a child. It was only after the splitting of Novu-Optu and the Borasian States that the wayward child would be cared for by their clan. It seems that Scor has lost their way but Thalkin, I promise you, Sal and I have not. Other families may do the bare minimum but while you are under this roof you will be treated as our own.' When she spoke, her eyes did not move away from Thalkin's.

She was smiling at Thalkin, but it did not make sense. 'Rosalind, please there is no need. I shall do what you need if you wish.' Thalkin felt anxious, there was an unfocused anger and nothing to release it upon. He gritted his teeth.

'Thalkin, you do not understand.'

'Rosalind, I do not need to. Within a few moons I shall be gone.' They stood in the garden in a tense silence, Thalkin not looking at Rosalind. 'Where is Sal's food and what do you need?'

Rosalind handed him some cloth with some bread, meat, cheese and honeyed cakes in and told him what she needed from the market. Thalkin made his way out, swinging his sack over his shoulder. He was tired and downhearted with the whole day still ahead of him. The town was bustling with activity by this time. People of all kinds were running through the streets, business was never far away from a street corner. A boy about his age, dressed finely bumped into Thalkin, cursing him as he ran past. He must have been a runner, a boy tasked with delivering messages for a merchant to his business partners and rivals across town. Thalkin looked after the boy as he walked on and thought about all the juicy secrets he would know. A baker was outside with his apprentice, organising a display. Thalkin walked past a smithy as he neared the centre of Scor, and he could feel the heat emanate from the inside of the opened hut. A powerfully built man, with dark hair tied loosely back, slammed a hammer down on the piece he was working on and then dropped it into a barrel full of water. The hiss and steam burst upwards. Thalkin knew the man to be Franka, said to be the best smith in town. Unfortunately, at the moment he was not making a weapon of any great value but a horseshoe instead, the bread and butter for most smiths. Franka raised the tongs that clasped the item he was working on and moved it into the light. The horseshoe looked perfect, so Franka placed it to one side and began working on another, hawking and spitting before slamming down on a fresh piece from the furnace.

As Thalkin was watching, a man walked into the smithy. He wore the garb of the town guard but Thalkin did not recognise him. He wasn't as big as Franka but he carried himself well; his walk was precise and he was light on his feet. There seemed to be a deadly agility about him, and he was by no means small. Thalkin could tell that beneath the chainmail and surcoat he was stronger than most. He was greying at the temples with military-styled short-cropped hair. Franka turned to him and looked at him passively. *Is that contempt in his eyes?* Thalkin mused. He watched with interest at the exchange but couldn't make out the whispers. The man's back was to Thalkin, so he could not see his lips move and Franka barely responded. The smith finally nodded and returned back to his work, spitting once again. Dark rings below his eyes clouded his face, showing his fatigue. Franka was a great blacksmith but as one of the few in town, he was extremely overworked at this time. The guard turned back to the street and Thalkin now got a look at the man. His eyes were sunken but sharp, he had a short, thick black beard with grey hairs spreading about it. A scar raked across his face and disfigured the end of his lip, giving him a permanent side sneer. His hand rested on the hilt of his blade as he jumped on a wagon that sat outside the smithy. The driver was another town guard, one that Thalkin knew well, Ranic. An ugly, vicious man whose aim was to make Thalkin's life as hard as possible. He regularly associated with Gregori and shared his aim to humiliate or hurt the orphan. He had slim features, stained teeth and flaking skin. He was covered in scabs from his skin condition and was seen scratching or picking his scabbing flesh when his hands were idle. However, he was a skilled fighter, with his only respite from the irritation being his sword practice. Thalkin had watched him train and, with bitter resentment conceded that Ranic was indeed skilled.

He had been watching Thalkin and grinned maliciously when the orphan's eyes fell on him. Thalkin glared, his anger rising once again. Ranic leant into the older fighter and whispered nodding in Thalkin's direction. The greying fighter turned but ignored Thalkin and made a motion for Ranic to exit the wagon. Ranic did as he was told and began unloading heavy crates from the wagon's rear. Franka helped, along with his apprentice whose name Thalkin did not know.

A snapping of fingers made Thalkin's eyes shoot to the driver's seat. Dark eyes stared at Thalkin. An emotionless, blank stare. The greying fighter leant ever so slightly in his seat and motioned Thalkin over. He did as he was told and made tentative steps towards the front of the wagon.

'I would keep myself out of other people's business, orphan.' There was a lack of emotion in the whisper that sent a chill through Thalkin, as those cold unblinking eyes left him in no doubt what would happen if he did not heed the advice without question.

Thalkin backed up, fear replacing the anger that had surfaced. His attention was now drawn to the back of the wagon. The grin that split Ranic's face made him look even uglier than normal. He carried a crate over to Franka's forge but was so focused on enjoying the threat directed at Thalkin that he wasn't watching his steps, and knocked into a passer-by. The crate slammed onto the floor, which split open with a clatter and something blinding fell out. The Father Sun had hit what looked like a sheet of pure steel. Thalkin only had a quick glimpse but it looked like chainmail except it wasn't connected together by small ringlets of metal. Instead, it was a smooth, singular piece of armour. A helmet bounced out as well which landed at

Thalkin's feet. He bent to pick it up for a closer look but the warrior next to Thalkin pushed him and gathered it up. He strode towards Ranic and struck him across the face with the back of his hand.

'If you don't want to be flayed within an inch of your life, put this away now,' he said in a quiet, menacing tone.

'Yes, Commander Billan.' Ranic bowed and the helmet was shoved hard into his stomach, knocking the wind out of him and bringing him to his knees. The helmet and armour was gathered quickly up and Ranic and Commander Billan looked around to see who was watching. Thalkin had made his exit and was looking at the scene from in between some passers-by. Thalkin had never seen armour like that before. The town guard wore a simple leather surcoat with the Scor crest on the chest and a coat of mail underneath. A helmet covered the side of the face with the nasal to cover the nose. This one, however, covered the whole face in iron with a slit for the eyes. Thalkin had seen mercenaries pass through town with varying styles of protection but not with armour such as that, and as far as Thalkin knew, it was the same for the whole of Duria.

Thalkin sped up to reach Sal, as he knew he was running a bit late, and started to daydream of wearing the armour himself. He pictured himself wearing it, slaying the people of Scor who occasionally hurt him. Thalkin sneered at that thought, as he imagined piercing the stomach of Gregori as the town burned around him. His thoughts then turned to Sal and Rosalind and he imagined rescuing them from being a slave to Lord Procterate Thomil and then burning the town down.

Lost in his daydreams, Thalkin found himself now on the outskirts of the town proper. The buildings began to space themselves out. A new street was rising from the ground in this area, joining buildings together, making them look like the inner town of Scor. Men moved stones, mixed mortar, slammed hammers, and chopped lumber as they set about the seemingly never-ending task of bloating up Scor. As much as Thalkin detested this town he could not stop marvelling at the machine that Thomil had created. Thalkin noticed two dome-shaped buildings with a chimney in the centre; one had not been completed yet and a furnace could be seen inside. Thalkin judged them to be forges that were much larger than Franka's smithy. A stable made from lumber was being constructed next to a larger building that looked to be an inn. A wall was being constructed around an open space with a two-storey building, made from pure blocks of stone. This was undoubtedly a marshalling yard for future guardsmen. There was another building which Thalkin had never seen before. It stood about sixty or seventy-foot-high with white pillars all the way around a square base, which were holding up a hip roof. There was an inner wall behind the pillars with a large entrance. It was certainly impressive but Thalkin had no inkling about what it was used for. All these buildings had men working on them, with apprentices running to and fro. He approached the workers with the intention of finding Sal.

'Where can I find Sal?' Thalkin asked a huge shirtless mason. The sun gleamed from the man's bald head as he churned the sand, lime and water to make the mortar. The mason stopped and looked Thalkin up and down before turning back to his work. 'Where can I find Sal?' he asked again. This time Thalkin was completely ignored. He never had any intention of moving on and asking someone else. Everything about the man angered Thalkin, from being ignored to the smell of stale sweat. He did not like this man so finding Sal became a second priority to organising a confrontation with the bald mason. 'Oaf, I asked a question.'

The mason dropped his spade that he was using to churn the mortar and turned to face Thalkin. He stood about 2 heads above Thalkin. He rolled his shoulders before asking 'Did I hear you make a sound, orphan?'

'No, but your mother---' Thalkin went to finish the insult but he was suddenly flying through the air. He landed with a thud on the earth, his ears ringing and his bottom lip already swelling up.

'What was you going to say, boy?' The mason loomed over him, nursing the back of the hand that had slapped Thalkin's lip.

Thalkin gritted his teeth and felt his jaw protest. He went to open his mouth when another voice came from somewhere.

'I believe he was going to say *your mother made quite a sound last night*, and for a boy of only fifteen years, I think that to be impressive.' Sal's voice calmly finished Thalkin's insult.

'Sal! Why do you defend this whore's mistake?' The mason laughed, turning to Sal who was now approaching the scene. Thalkin propped himself up on one elbow and saw that several others had stopped their work to watch the commotion.

'Because, Strannin, he is under my care, as is the custom of the Borasian states. Or had you forgotten?' Sal walked straight up to the mason, Strannin, until only an inch or two separated them. Sal was broad and tall but Strannin had a few inches on him.

Strannin snarled at Sal but simply shrugged and went back to his work. Thalkin was trying to stand when he felt a hand lift him up. The hand moved to his shoulder and led him away from the scene. They sat down on an unfinished wall and Thalkin spat blood. Sal pushed a jug of water in Thalkin's hand, it was cold.

'For your lip.' Sal sat quietly as Thalkin winced pressing the cold jug against his swelling lip. 'You are tough, Thalkin, not many people could take a hit from Strannin.'

'I've had bigger men and women hit me harder,' he mumbled.

'You have my food, I see.'

Thalkin took off his bag and handed it to Sal, who grunted his thanks. He began biting into the food that Rosalind had prepared. He tore off some bread and handed it to Thalkin. He put the water down, and with some difficulty, began to chew. Sal drank deeply from the water jug, wiping Thalkin's blood off the rim with a small piece of cloth he had in a back pocket of his work breeches. They ate in silence for a minute before Sal started the conversation back up.

'I mentioned earlier that you have fifteen years. Is this correct?' Sal asked with his mouth full.

'Aye, if anyone is counting.'

Sal nodded his understanding. 'Have you thought about what you would do? In Renlac, the child gets to choose the profession he wants to pursue, and is not bound by his family's tradition. They experience many things in their youth, and are already apprentice to so many trades. Yet I am guessing you have not worked much with your families.'

Thalkin just nodded.

'So, what do you know?'

Thalkin shrugged. 'Nothing.' Sal just looked at Thalkin. 'I know how to fish, climb, run, I know my letters, and how to spy, listen, and take a punch,' Thalkin smirked 'and throw one.'

Sal smiled at that. 'I'm guessing you didn't learn any of this from the families you stayed with?' Thalkin shook his head.

'From early on, I learned that the only chance I had to survive was to bargain my invisibility to this town. They had secrets from each other, desires and demands. I helped in exchange for knowledge.' Thalkin had finished his bread and so had Sal.

Sal shook his head. 'It is not an unknown thing for this to happen, where cities are concerned, but such disregard in a town of this size surprises me.'

Thalkin was looking away, his back bent low as he leant on his knees. He was clenching and unclenching his jaw, feeling the pain from the strike.

'It won't be long before you choose, you must think on this,' Sal said.

Thalkin did not understand why Sal and Rosalind cared so much. He was doing fine at this point. He always thought about travelling, moving away from Scor, but had no money to achieve this. Thinking on it only caused despair and panic for Thalkin, so he never dwelt on it for long. Today had been long and now seemed longer because of these questions. He stood up suddenly as he started to feel the panic rise in him. 'Things are different here in Scor, Sal. I am unsure of my future and I doubt I'll be in this town for much longer.' He was unsure of what more to say so Thalkin nodded his leave to Sal who watched him walk away before heading back to work.

The market in the centre of Scor was thick with noise and activity. It was considered to be the heart of the town and all roads converged there. Scor was built on a gentle hill that overlooked the surrounding land. The roads all gently rose up so once at the top one could see the town below, as well as the open plains surrounding it. Traders set up their stalls around a water fountain and raised their voices in a cacophony of noise. It was just past midday, so the sun was beating down its summer heat. Some children were splashing in the fountain whilst their mothers went from stall to stall, picking up exotic wares that could not be found in the established stores of Scor. Merchants shouted out their lungs, expressing how only they could sell the most unique and affordable objects from around the world. There was even some fruit that Thalkin had never seen before on a stall with a small disorderly mob around it, that was so busy a disgruntled town guard was having to direct the flow of patrons. The merchant, on the other hand, was beaming with joy as his stock depleted rapidly. Thalkin scanned the hips of the bustling crowd and could see a few coin purses that could easily be snatched. He had been taught the skill of pickpocketing from a town guard who wanted to know the exact time when certain store owners closed their shops up and retreated to their beds. Unfortunately for him he was stabbed by Dravis, the owner of a successful pottery shop, who had been having trouble sleeping and caught this guard trying to steal from his home. Thalkin had not only learned how to pick-pocket from that town guard that night, but also never to steal from a potter who had trouble sleeping. Thalkin thought better of trying his hand at the purses that dangled so temptingly, remembering Sal and Rosalind's words. At the moment, he was in a good household, until he had to leave within a few moons, so he would not cause them any bother, like he had in so many other households he had been forced to stay with.

He looked at the list Rosalind had prepared for him and began to pick up some items, most of which were available at the stores of Scor. However, there were a few that could only be found here. He would pick up the local items in the town's stores on his way back but thought that, with the fever that sometimes takes hold of people in the marketplace, he wanted to get these items out of the way now. He made use of his slight, small frame and pushed his way through to the front of the mobs, picking what he needed and paying with the money Rosalind had given him. He even haggled with some of the stall owners and managed to save Rosalind some draub copper. He avoided the stall owners who had more of a permanent residence in the town square as they would accuse him of stealing, pickpocketing or simply being a filthy orphan. He would have argued at any objections being placed upon him, but he was not in the mood to deal with any grief this day.

As he finished circling the square, he passed the Flayed Dragon and saw Momo sitting outside with a skin of some unknown liquid. He was smiling as if he had just been told some hilarious joke. He no longer wore his headscarf and Momo's hair hung loosely down his shoulders. He was not bald, after all, but to be fair did have a receding line. His hair was grey with odd lines of black running through it and wore it like most men of Kytosh did, in thick, tight braids. Thalkin smiled as he walked over. He did not know much of Kytosh, as it was a far northern kingdom, so he was excited to learn more about one of the three free kingdoms from the odd traveller.

'How fare you, Momo?' Thalkin asked leaning on the wall next to him.

He had not been looking at Thalkin as he approached him but did not appear to be startled at the question. 'Very, very good, Thalkin. Yourself?' He asked, handing the water skin to Thalkin.

Thalkin took a sip and a fruity, full-flavored, dark wine filled his mouth. Thalkin coughed in surprise but took another sip. 'Not bad, although I don't think my taste buds are awake to appreciate it.'

'Of that I am sure. It was late for a child such as you to be out.'

'I am no child.'

Momo nodded, looking at Thalkin for the first time, his yellowed teeth beaming at him. 'Well, what brings you to the market?'

Thalkin tapped his bag. 'Just making my rounds.'

'Of course. It's a wonderful place isn't it.' He took a deep breath. 'Can you smell it, Thalkin?'

Thalkin sniffed. 'Sweat? Dung? Bread?'

'Money.' He beamed. 'Look at them, this town is small but in a few tennights it shall be a city and it shall truly grow then. It is when you will truly make money. The first city which will govern its own state, Thalkin, for hundreds of years. Something special is happening here and I am going to be a part of it.' Momo talked excitedly, his eyes wild as he looked at the scene before him and Thalkin was certain they were seeing two different things. 'When that Thomil is declared the official Lord Procterate of Scor, it will all change.' His eyes were darting about as if he was seeing the town change before his very eyes.

Thalkin did not say anything, he couldn't imagine his life getting any better. He was aware of the festivities being planned when the delegation of Borasian States arrived in the future to declare Scor independent of Tyton, but did not care much for it. No official date had been set, although it was agreed it was just a matter of time, which was all the more reason for him to be ignored. He decided to change the subject. 'What I fail to understand, Momo, is you are merchant are you not?'

Momo nodded with emphasis.

'So why are you not out there, selling whatever it is you brought from Kytosh?' Thalkin nodded toward the chaos of the marketplace.

Momo smiled 'Kalai always taught that patience is key to winning in battle. Buying and selling goods is a battle, so I am being patient.'

Thalkin frowned with annoyance at the enigmatic answer that, referenced the long-dead general of the North. 'Surely, you need to make yourself known to the people so they will keep coming to you day after day?'

'Timing over speed,' Momo replied secretly again. Thalkin clicked his tongue. It did not pass Momo's notice. 'When this town is finally declared a state of Boras, there'll be a lot of celebration, will there not?'

Thalkin just looked at Momo.

'People tend to spend their coins when they are in abundance and being happy or drunk doesn't hurt, and neither does being happy and drunk with an abundance of coin.' Momo slapped his knee as he laughed at his joke.

Thalkin sighed. 'You are only going to answer me with riddles, aren't you?'

'Secrets and rumour spread quicker than the truth.'

Thalkin's annoyance was turning to anger. 'Good day to you, Momo.' He went to walk away.

Momo chuckled at Thalkin's annoyance and motioned for the boy to come back. 'Thalkin, I have a quest for you, in exchange I shall tell you the secret of my wares.'

Thalkin turned, his anger now subsiding and a new excitement building. 'What do you wish of me?' he asked, smiling ruefully.

Momo smirked. 'There is a merchant who's space I would like. If there is a way you can get him to move, I shall tell you about my wares.'

'Ah, so that is why you are sitting here and not at the stalls.' Thalkin thought for a bit but shook his head. 'Not good enough.'

'You don't understand. You shall know my secret because I shall gift you one.' Momo rubbed his hands together, looking at Thalkin eagerly.

Thalkin thought about it, Momo's wares could be useless to him, but then again, they could be of great value. Also, his work with Edgir had ended for the moment so there was little else he would be doing. Weighing the risk against reward, he decided it would be worth it, no matter what Momo's merchandise was. 'Who is the merchant you wish me to move?'

Momo snapped his fingers and chuckled again. He took a gulp of wine and beckoned for Thalkin to sit. 'He goes by the name of Pickfill Grannin, he sells—'

'Meats, the hunters sell their skin and meats to him. He deals in smaller game, such as rabbits, foxes and birds. Maybe boar.' Thalkin rubbed his chin, his mind already working.

'I need this done within a tennight. It is very important.'

Thalkin thought about it. 'How do I know your wares are worth it?'

'They are worth more than gold my young friend.'

Thalkin scoffed at this but finally shrugged. 'Fine Momo, you have a deal.' Thalkin held out his forearm and Momo took it.

'Nine days.' And then he said no more, leaning back against the wall, sipping at his wineskin.

Thalkin moved away. Feeling very tired, he was tempted to walk back to Sal's and Rosalind's house. He felt like he could sleep the whole day away and certainly planned to, yet he still had a few more errands to run. So he trudged along, looking forward to collapsing in his temporary bed.

Chapter Three

Signs were being brought in, the taverns beginning to fill, and the candlelight from the windows was making the shadows dance in the street. A light drizzle brought out the smells of spring as Scor was finishing another day. The days were still getting longer and the town was turning into a frenzy as people flocked to Scor. It felt like something was going to happen soon, rumours were buzzing in the corners of the taverns and along the street as people shopped and gossiped. For hundreds of years, the Thomil family had tried to both grow Scor and free it from the control of Tyton. Fortunately, Tyton had never wanted the responsibility. It just drained some of the money drawn from its lucrative trade route and farms. The other Borasian states thought Tyton would be too powerful, so when the first Free Lord Procterates divided the land, they overstretched Tyton for the balance of the other states. With Thomil's ever-increasing friendship with the elves of the Veil and dwarves of the Yangzte Empire and easy access to the trade between Vadir, Tyton and the Veil, it made sense to make Scor its own state. This kept Tyton dependent on Scor for trade routes while not gifting Scor to another state and upsetting the balance of power that had lasted for centuries.

Through the drizzle a lean, dark merchant pulled a small wagon down the muddened street. His hair was tied back with a loose strand that passed over his clean-shaven face. He pulled the small horseless wagon with some ease as it was only a quarter full, demonstrating another successful day for Pickfill Grannin. His mind must have been elsewhere, either that or Thalkin was well hidden, because he did not turn his head to the alley that the young orphan skulked in. Thalkin let out a breath of frustration. He had been shadowing the merchant for several days since Momo's request but had, alas, discovered nothing about him. This was partly due to the lack of effort he was putting in. He had begrudgingly agreed to not come home late anymore whilst staying with Sal and Rosalind. The repetition of Thalkin's days was a comforting change in lifestyle for him. He would wake early and eat with Sal and Rosalind and then tend the garden with the woman from Renlac. After this, he would have some time for himself, in which he tried to gather any information he could on Pickfill. Nothing of worth had turned up in his spying. He had, at various times of the day, lingered around the stall operated by Pickfill whose booming voice almost drowned out the bustle of the constantly busy square. There was always a crowd around his stall, not only was it situated in the heart of the marketplace but his meats were so fresh and delicious, there was always a high demand for them. He never had to salt them, as his hunters were coming with fresh game in a constant stream. The animals were freshly butchered and drained whenever he was running low in the day, which was a common occurrence. Listening in on conversations, Thalkin heard that the people around Scor found it strange that Pickfill had never owned a store but instead disappeared from the town at random points in the year for several days. This grain of information was all that Thalkin could go on. It seemed that Pickfill's only relationships were with his hunters, which considering how charming he was, certainly seemed strange.

Thalkin stuck to the roads, avoiding his worn boots from clunking on the wooded walkways. They were heading north towards the home of the mysterious, charming merchant. The road opened up to the west and Thalkin could see the mountain that overlooked the ambitious town. Nestled in the face of the gradual slope of the mountain was the Keep of Scor, an ancient residue of the Elvish Kingdom. Its name lost to antiquity. The turrets were broad at the base and slimmed down as they rose up, like silent sentinels of the past. Black spikes of stone jutted out from the towers, which must have served some unknown defensive purpose. The walls took the same design; thick at the base, they sloped upwards and thinned out at the top. The trees and the overgrowth were now staking their claim as wardens of the Keep. Even with the close relationship that Scor had shared with the Elves of the Veil, they still held the secrets of the world close to their chest. It didn't require an urchin, who prided himself on his ability to acquire knowledge, to know this. The elves, who faced near extinction, guarded the history of the world like it was the only land they had left.

Thalkin in his musing almost lost his quarry but was quickly back on track after he regained his focus. Pickfill had been looking behind him while Thalkin had stared at the Keep, so paid him no heed as he stopped outside his home. Pickfill pulled the wagon round the side and began to stack the small amount of unsold goods with long sinewy arms and made his way into his home. Thalkin knew this part of town. There was a cluster of trees several yards away, which he could reach by going around the back of a home that faced Pickfill's house, so as not to be seen. He climbed up and thanks to the end of spring, the tree was full of coloured leaves, hiding him from view. He looked through the gold and red, of the white birch tree and took the building into account. It was a small and humble affair, which looked like it was only big enough for one or two people. Made of dark timber, the roof had moss on it to help with the insulation and there was only one window to the right of the door, where a light could be seen. Smoke was rising from the chimney, which meant that Pickfill had lit the fire. The smell of meat being cooked made its way to Thalkin, and his belly growled. He took the bread and cheese he had taken from Rosalind's kitchen and tore into it.

He waited some time for any activity around the house. Every so often someone would come walking past and Thalkin would watch them eagerly, trying to see who they were. He took a mental note of their faces and placed a name on most of them, but they all innocently walked past the shack. His excitement with each passer-by dwindled until, as the sun was setting and the shadows lay long on the ground, Thalkin saw two men come into view from behind the shack. There was a group of homes that lay beyond a small field and pond, which the two men seemed to appear from. Beyond these houses were the woods that most of the town's game was found. The road north to Tyton skirted this wood, so it was fairly well known to the people of Scor, but few ventured into it because of the simple dangers that any moderately sized woodland area provided. There were no centigorgons or arachnataurs, but boars and the odd bear that only the most masterful of hunters could take down, or avoid in most cases. The two men had their hoods up and looked over their shoulders as they made their way towards Pickfill's hut. Thalkin remained patient but his excitement started to grow again. It seemed like ages since he'd had his last adventure. To be fair, it had only been a short time since the last time he'd been out spying and skulking around, but his promise to Sal and Rosalind made it feel like an eternity. His promise had almost made him feel guilty for sitting in the tree and spying, almost. There must have been a back entrance because Thalkin heard a rap on wood followed by a haste-filled voice. There was a creak and then a slam.

Thalkin tapped his fingers on the tree, deciding if anyone else would arrive. He scanned the street, it seemed quiet and tranquil. This might be his only chance to find anything out, but if he was caught any chance of coming back was gone, and yet if he didn't move now, any information that he needed might be gone too. He made his mind up and dropped from the tree, landing like a cat. He fixed his cloak and put his hood up. The sky was darkening now in earnest. He made his way around the back, casting another look across the field in case another conspirator was making their way. The insects of the night were starting to awaken in the field, but apart from that, there was nothing. He crept around and placed his ear to the door and heard voices. They were too muffled so he pushed it open slightly, it creaked but the voices continued, louder this time.

'We need more, Pickfill!'

'I cannot increase your supply, what I held in reserve has been exhausted. The increase of people has meant the demand has increased you will just have to make do!'

'You don't understand, I can't even hunt without it now, I feel naked, as if my bow is unstrung.'

There were three voices, Pickfill's was the same, crisp and loud; however, it was lacking the charm and there was a slight strain. The two other voices, were raspy, quiet and edgy.

'Once you have Breath, Pickfill your focus without it does not exist. I only have enough left for maybe two or three more days.'

'The same for me and the other lads.'

'You have just built up a need for it. I was promised that it just helped with a man's focus, you will lose your desire for it and be back to normal.'

'Some of us have died, Pickfill!'

The voice almost screeched. Pickfill hushed him.

'Listen, my friend, the person who gave me this concoction of Breath swore to me, that on his good name no one can die when leaving it behind. It will hurt, of course, but you will live and be stronger for it, and probably become better hunters.'

'It is not only that. The game. It's drying up.' Another voice entered now, deeper but still strained, almost fearful.

'What, how? Go deeper into the woods then.'

'We are already deep, there is six of us going in there every day. The animals are moving. Soon there will be no game in those woods. It should be fine for this year---'

'So what is the problem, then?'

'It is getting more difficult to track what is left, that's why we need more.'

There was silence.

'After we run out, Pickfill I don't think any of us will be in any state to supply you.'

'Then I shall find someone else. It was a mistake trusting you, and your gang, leave me at once. I shall find other hunters and ones who don't need Breath.'

Some chairs slowly scraped on the floor and Thalkin heard the sound of iron rasping from leather.

'Now put that away lads, I was only jesting, I am tired. The weight of the night and this business is just getting to me, that is all.'

'Listen, it seems you are missing the point. We aren't asking, we are telling. We need more, and you are going to get it. Now.'

'I can't get it now, he is not in Scor. I must ride, it will take me a few days.'

'Well, that's just in time for us to run out. Sounds perfect to me.'

'Yes, and me.'

The edgy voices were lower now, menacing. Thalkin could almost hear them sneering as they spoke.

'What about my stall? I hear Thomil is due to make an announcement. It will be a huge day, people will have need for my stall.'

'Well, you best get riding then, you will probably make it back in time. And I'm sure you know someone who can take over for a day or two, maybe me or one of the lads can do it. What do you think?' The two hunters spoke in a mocking friendly tone.

'Oh Pickfill, not to worry we'll take care of your home while you are away.' Their words were hardly soothing, even Thalkin could hear the venom in their voices.

'I think he's got the message, come on, let's go.'

Thalkin heard the blade being re-sheathed and then footsteps moved toward him. As quietly as he could, he made for the street, making sure he couldn't be seen from any of the windows of Pickfill's shack.

His mind began to work, he had obviously found something that could now be used against Pickfill, but how? He was away for a few days so Momo could take his spot, but then Pickfill would return in two days anyway. Maybe Thalkin could steal the Breath, whatever that was, from the hunters by forcing some confrontation. This could lead to Pickfill being killed, which didn't sit too well with Thalkin. However, he wasn't totally against the idea to be fair. Moreover, there were too many aspects to the plan that Thalkin did not know about. Where were the men hiding? What did Breath look like? What was Breath? It was definitely some form of concoction, and finding out exactly what it was felt like a good first step. Thalkin looked up at the sky and saw he still had maybe an hour or two before his promise to Rosalind and Sal would be broken. He decided to make his way to Edgir, as he was the best person Thalkin could think of asking.

He found himself on Edgir's street, which was quiet and deserted. The only sign of life was coming from the window of the only habited house on the street, as a candlelight flickered inside. Thalkin noticed smoke billowing from the chimney, strange as the old fighter rarely had his hearth blazing. As he drew near, he heard voices from the inside, one voice belonging to Edgir and one he had never heard before. He knocked on the door and was told to enter.

'Ah Thalkin, please sit.' Edgir gestured toward a chair. Edgir was standing next to the fire, his skin looking less yellow now and he had an uncharacteristic smile on his face. The few strands of hair that clung to his head sat neatly slicked back. He still looked a mess, but a mess that had been piled into a corner, and so had some resemblance of order. Leaning against a side table was a woman. She had her white hair tied back into a single plat, that hung over her shoulder. She had a wrinkled, weather-beaten face. Her eyes were dark, like pools of ink tinged with brown around the edge. They regarded Thalkin unblinkingly. Her arms were folded across her chest and she wore brown leather riding boots with padded trousers tucked into them. She still wore her cloak despite the warmth, underneath it was a leather vest with a mail hauberk that hung below her waist. Hanging from her left side a sheathed hand and a half-sword hilt poked out with a dagger on the right. There was a dangerous stillness about her. Thalkin looked back at Edgir whose eyes were darting between the traveller and Thalkin.

'I have something to ask you.' Thalkin said turning to Edgir, aware of the two pairs of eyes staring at him. 'I need to know about Breath.'

Edgir's eyes flickered and his brow furrowed. 'Breath, why Thalkin?' Suspicion was etched on his face.

'It's not for me,' Thalkin replied waving his hand. 'I need to know about it, what exactly is it? Where does it come from?'

'It is not a world you should enter, Thalkin,' said Edgir, who actually looked concerned.

'Let the boy know,' the woman said. Each word was measured, evenly spaced.

'Edelia, I'm not sure---'

'It is a concoction of varying types.' She cut him off, a hint of impatience in her voice. 'Its use is strictly forbidden in all realms of man.'

Thalkin's heart skipped a beat. He knew from Pickfill's conversation with the hunters that its use would have to be a secret. 'Why is it forbidden?'

'You shall not tell the boy,' Edgir told the woman known as Edelia. She looked lazily at him. 'I don't care, I will not tell him this.' Edgir folded his arms.

'Why is it so bad?' Thalkin was taken aback by Edgir's concern.

'Why do you want to know?' Edelia looked straight into Thalkin's eyes as she asked him the question, shifting her weight on her seat, her weapons knocking slightly on the wood.

'For reasons of my own. I am asking Edgir not you.' Thalkin didn't like how this old woman was imposing herself into his business, and it also unsettled him how she was treating Edgir.

'Well, you are at an impasse. Edgir will not tell you. I will, but only if you indulge my curiosity.' They stared at each other. She opened her arms 'What will it be, Thalkin?' There was a slight smirk on her face, which annoyed Thalkin.

He sighed, however, and said, 'I am on an errand for someone, whose name I shall not speak of and whose errand I shall not tell. Tonight, I have been presented a possible solution to my task, but I need information. This information could give leverage to the person I am helping.'

Edelia nodded, her smile widening. She then looked at Edgir with a look of...approval, was it?

'OK, Breath, as I said comes in different forms. It was initially used to relax muscles, helping field surgeons to cut limbs off wounded soldiers, or to help their passing. After the Schism and the dust settled, men found another use for Breath. It puts you in a state of total euphoria when it's used in large quantities. However, it has one big side effect, it becomes a parasite. For Breath to work, it consumes your body in order to assist its purpose, and because the effects are so good, people become dependent on it and you eventually waste away.'

'Why would anyone do that?'

Edelia shrugged. 'Many reasons. However, there are other uses for it. It was soon discovered it could also harness a man's focus, make him stronger, faster. Men I know used it in battle to give them an edge as it would dull their pain. It also had its drawbacks as the men would take wounds in battle and let them go unnoticed, so they would drop dead because of the infection that had rooted itself in the cut. It is called Breath simply because of the way it is administered. The power of the concoction comes from its vapours. You simply hover over the pot, or vial, and take a big lungful of air and that's it.' Edelia laid out her hands. 'That is all I know.'

'And because of that, it is forbidden?'

'Give a man an easy way to become greater than he already is and he'll take it, no matter what the cost. Or give him an escape when everything has been taken from him...' She shrugged again letting her sentence hang in the air.

'Not all men,' Edgir said.

'Nor women,' Edelia smiled.

'Aye, I understand.' Thalkin nodded, his mind ticking.

'So Thalkin, you are not thinking of using the concoction, are you?' Edgir asked, shifting in his seat and leaning forward.

Thalkin shook his head. 'Of course not, Edgir. What I said was true. I must go now, I have to see someone and I have little time to do it.' He turned to leave but before he could, Edgir called him back.

'Thalkin, there was something I wanted to ask of you too.' He turned to Edelia, who nodded. 'Edelia is an old friend who also has a task and I think you'd be perfect for it.'

'What does Edelia want me to do that she cannot ask me herself?' Thalkin spoke to Edgir but he could see Edelia out the corner of his eye, and she was still staring right at him.

'Well, as you know things are changing in Scor. It's becoming a state of its own. Rumours are it'll be declared in a few days and an official ceremony will take place in a few months.' Edelia interrupted with a cough, Edgir looked to reconsider his words. 'You have to promise that what we discuss does not leave this room.'

Thalkin cocked his head to one side. 'Edgir, you shame me.'

Edgir held up his hands 'Fair enough, boy. Fair enough. Fine, I shall not tell you all the details only what you need to know. There is something about this town that is more famous than its wine, ale, and it being an important trade route. For hundreds of years the Borasian States have stood at six, and now Scor is becoming the seventh State. Many are questioning why, especially people in the North.'

'Novu-Optu?' Thalkin's mouth dropped. 'Are you from the Godlands?' he looked straight at Edelia.

She stood up and strode towards the candle in the window and extinguished the flame with her finger and thumb, gazing outside at the street. 'I am not from anywhere, but some say I am everywhere.'

Thalkin rolled his eyes and closed his mouth, turning back to Edgir.

'It does not matter where Edelia is from, what is important is that people are willing to pay to know what makes Scor and more specifically Thomil, so important.'

Thalkin's eyes narrowed at the mention of Boldon Thomil, whose son made Thalkin's life a living hell. 'So, where do I fit in?'

'I have told Edelia of your abilities.' He made a motion with his hand, passing the conversation over to the mysterious Edelia.

'Thomil lives outside the town centre, does he not?' Edelia asked from behind Thalkin, making him turn in his seat.

'He does, on his farm.'

'Describe it.' Edelia left the window and came to sit opposite Thalkin in an empty chair and once again looked straight into his eyes, studying him.

'It stretches many hides of land, there are grapes, pears, apples, corn, wheat, pigs, cows, sheep. He harvests anything. He has the biggest farm, with a finger or two in the others and most of the goods are touched by his hand. The farm is large but unremarkable. What is of interest is how he lives. He has a large house in which all his business is conducted. This house sits at the bottom of a road, the road is lined with his closest advisors' homes. This area is well guarded, and his most loyal and long-standing farm hands double up as his personal guard and patrol this road in the night, swapping watches as the night marches into daylight.'

'He already has his own government, it seems,' Edelia said thoughtfully, looking away now.

'He does, a much shrewder man than me, I must admit. It is why I lost everything,' Edgir said with sadness. Thalkin had not seen this side of Edgir before. In fact, when Thalkin looked around, there was not an empty bottle to be seen, nor was the smell of brewing spirits in the air.

'Indeed,' is all that Edelia said to this. 'How do you know all this, Thalkin?'

'Well, I have spied on him. For Edgir mostly.'

'Aye, you did lad.' Edgir smiled. A rare sight.

'So, you know your way around, you could sneak in again?' Edelia leant forward, one hand resting on the chair, the other on the hilt of her sword.

'If need be.'

'Well, there is a need.' She stood up now, her eyes deep in thought, which reminded Thalkin a little of himself. She snapped herself out of her revere. 'Edgir I shall speak to you soon. I must make plans, plans concerning our mutual friend here.'

'Wait, I have not agreed to anything.' Thalkin felt a surge of annoyance.

Edelia turned and with a smirk that Thalkin had already grown to hate, said, 'Oh, you will.' And with that, she was out the door.

'Edgir, what is going on?' Thalkin asked.

Edgir rose from his chair to watch Edelia walk away into the darkness, checking if anyone was following her. 'This is it Thalkin, my comeback and you, my boy, will help!' He sounded excited, alive. He put his hand on Thalkin's shoulder. 'Silver, gold and a promise of revenge. This is the first step. Thomil has something. The Thomil family has always been the strongest in Scor, with no competitors for decades. I was the last. Suddenly, the Lord Procterates vote for Scor to become a State?' He moved away, rubbing his hand against his freshly shaven face. 'We need to find out why and then inform Edelia, she will use that information to crush him.'

'You trust this woman? She looks like a sellsword, Edgir' Thalkin said with blatant suspicion.

'I don't trust anyone. Alas, Edelia is a woman of repute,' he grinned. 'The tales that follow her.' Edgir then looked off, his gaze a thousand miles away.

Thalkin looked at the door that Edelia had exited from. *Who was this, Edelia?* he thought. 'Fair enough, but she actually told you this was to bring Thomil down? That is a big promise to make.'

'No, of course not. She promised me---us. Promised us silver, Thalkin. You will get a share too. To live your own life, to escape Scor for good. What has this hole of a town ever given you, and you now have the chance to make the first blow against it.'

Edgir said what Thalkin had always dreamt of but it was all so sudden for him. He had learnt to be more cautious than this. Thalkin put up his hands. 'Edgir, please. We don't even know what she wants me to do yet. You have taught me things Edgir, but I have learnt some things on my own. I could do with some silver, but I am not agreeing to anything yet.' Thalkin turned to leave and put his hand on the door handle.

'Speak to Ranic, he needs to get in favour with the new commander. He'll help you solve your little quest,' Edgir said bitterly to Thalkin's back.

Thalkin turned to give him Edgir his thanks, but he was already lumbering into the kitchen of the dilapidated house. Thalkin sighed and stepped into the cool air, shivering as he left the warmth of Edgir's living room. He pulled his cloak around him tightly, looking up at the stars. He knew he had broken his promise, but it was too late to care, he was off to find Ranic.

Chapter Four

Thalkin spent some time looking for Ranic. He wasn't even sure if he was on duty but he had to be informed tonight. Pickfill would have to leave town for a few days to acquire more supplies and in the meantime, his concoction-dependent hunters would take care of his stall. Ranic would be able to identify everyone involved and tail Pickfill and whoever went into the woods to hunt for game. Of course, Thalkin wasn't going to give this information freely, as it was immensely valuable to the young guardsmen and now he had a new commander it would be a sure way to get him on his good side. Thalkin decided to head for the town centre, as there was always someone on guard duty around the Flayed Dragon.

He came out upon the town square which even now, as the Spring Moon peaked through and pierced the clouds streaking them with moonlight, there was some activity. Outside the Flayed Dragon Inn a teamster readied his two chestnut beasts of burden, whilst the merchant whose goods were strapped down on the cart behind, checked the lashings, making sure that his livelihood was secure. Two guards were leaning on their spears as they watched a drunk they had just roused from a doorway on the other side, their laughter turning to steam against the cold air.

The stalls were being broken down, now they were done with today's business. However, not long before, this square had been a boom of business and activity, with chatter about price cuts and once-in-a-lifetime goods. Thalkin had underestimated the time he had taken. The nights were drawing ever shorter and the street urchin felt a knot of worry in his stomach. Rosalind and Sal would not be happy with him now. He had broken his promise and for what? A silly game for a man who he didn't even know. Yet he couldn't stop, he couldn't turn back now that it was almost at an end.

Thalkin eyed Pickfill's stall. No one was there. His eyes then moved towards The Flayed Dragon, expecting to see Momo surveying the activity, but he was nowhere to be seen. What truly piqued his interest was the robed man who stood upon the fountain that sat in the middle of the circled centre of town. The water looked painfully cold yet the man still stood atop it with his hands raised high. His robe was a dull red colour, with a simple hemp rope tied around his mid-drift. He wore plain sandals and had no other protection against the cold. Thalkin shivered merely looking at him.

As he watched, a man passed Thalkin from the direction of the robed man, who he recognised as one of the masons who worked with Sal.

'Excuse me, sir?'

He was new to the town, so he did not treat Thalkin with the same contempt as the townsfolk. 'Yes?'

'Who is that man?'

'A priest or madman, chanting about prophecies and the end of the world.' He scoffed when he replied 'The old Gods eh. Too late in the day for that.' He nodded to Thalkin and made his way home.

It seemed that the priest had just finished a sermon as he was dipping his head into the fountain, looking like he was drinking from it. Thalkin pulled a face, he had been thirsty many a night but he was never so thirsty as to drink from the water fountain. Thalkin moved towards the guardsmen who were looking tired as they leant on their spears. The drunk had moved on and their smiles had turned into yawns. One of them noticed Thalkin as he approached them.

'Off with you, Thalkin. We don't want any pockets being snatched at the end of our watch.'

'There aren't pockets to snatch, my dear guardsmen,' Thalkin said overly disappointedly.

'Well, clear off anyway. We have only an hour to go before we turn in our shift.'

'You have certainly deserved some rest most would say, that drunk was a threat to us all.'

'Watch it, son of a whore.' The guard was in no mood for jokes.

Thalkin's skin pricked with anger. He heard a spluttering behind him, which sounded like the priest had fallen in the water but he was too angry to look. His eyes bore into the guardsmen who stared right back. 'Where is Ranic?'

The guard looked confused. 'What do you want with him?'

'If you don't tell me where Ranic is, I'll make sure that every time you are on third watch you won't be able to stand still, I'll have you running around the town so much.'

'Just tell him, I tire of his presence,' The other guard said yawning.

'Fine, it's nothing to me anyway, it'd be nice to see that little rat Ranic kept busy by you. He's at the southern pass, checking over travellers from Vadir.'

Thalkin spat his thanks at their feet, hoping they would give chase but he heard only taunts about his unknown mother and father. With his back to the guardsmen, he looked towards where the priest stood but there was no one, only vendors who were finishing closing down from today's business. Thalkin shrugged and turned southwards.

He walked quickly, vainly attempting to reduce the trouble he was in when he returned to his momentary home. He thought about how Rosalind would shame him, call him worthless and an oath breaker, shred her veil of mock compassion, and eventually kick him out, while Sal looked on with wordless disappointment, grabbing Thalkin by the scruff off the neck and slapping him across the face for good measure. Thalkin didn't care, he didn't need them. He was having fun. Sneaking, spying, bartering, he lived for this. With that thought his belly rumbled and he realised how hungry he was. He turned a corner and walked right into something solid and, felt something wet connect with his face. He shook his head and looked up into a pair of wild, dark eyes. Shaggy, thin, curly hair drooped over a sunken, gaunt face. A patchy uneven beard surrounded a thin mouth with crooked teeth, that shook as if something was bubbling inside, fighting to come out. It was the priest and his white hair was dripping wet onto his dirty red robes.

'Sorry, I wasn't watching where I was going.' Thalkin stared unsure of what he was looking at.

'The darkness, lies in all of us. You know this.' The priest stammered. Thalkin was unsure if he was shivering or just mad.

'Indeed. I'll be on my way, now.'

Thalkin went to move around him, but the priest's hand shot out, and with a vice grip, squeezed the street urchin's arm.

'It brings the light, that's its most powerful weapon. Deception. It will cover the world with brightness, whilst infecting us with the shadows. So long as there is light there is darkness!' The priest had his other hand on Thalkin's shoulder now, and his thin fingers dug into Thalkin. Spittle sat on his lips until it shot off, hitting Thalkin in the face, while horrid breath crept into his nostrils and made his face twist with disgust. He tried to fight back, but the strength of the priest was surprisingly unrelenting.

'Unhand me priest. Your breath is infecting me!'

'Look at me, boy!' The priest's fingers relented and slowly he pulled them away, but Thalkin could not move. Instead, the man's wild, dark eyes bore into Thalkin's. Something was in there, Thalkin felt it. It was hard to explain but for a few moments two voices spoke inside his head. The orphan felt his mind being probed like someone rifling through pages in a book. The voices were not in a language that he could comprehend but there were indeed two voices. One sounded like the priest, but calmer, and the other was filled with authority, a voice that held both wisdom and power. Suddenly the voices left his head and the grip loosened. The priest stepped away and Thalkin's focus came back. He realised he had been looking up at the sky. The priest's insane look was back, his eyes darted from side to side and he tugged on his scruffy beard, an action that would normally be a thoughtful gesture but he was pulling some hairs out. 'We'll be seeing each other soon.' He walked and pushed past Thalkin.

The orphan felt weak and dazed by the encounter. He wanted to shout and chase the priest but his head started to pound. After some vigorous rubbing, the pain started to subside. The priest was far from gone. He made a note, if he ever saw that priest again he would kick him in the knackers. His legs almost buckled as he started to run south but it didn't take long for him to regain full control. As he ran, he thought about the voices in his head. It must have been some trick, Thalkin had heard about priests being able to cast Shimmer. On second thoughts, if he saw the priest again he would avoid him at all costs. Either way he didn't have time to dwell on the dishevelled mad man.

The buildings became increasingly sparse as Thalkin entered the outskirts of the town. He spotted the wooden tower that marked the edge of Scor, which served as the gatehouse for visitors. Thirty feet it rose up with a single watchman who stood atop it. There were two horses saddled up and two guardsmen issuing the steady traffic that made its way into town. Ranic was leaning on the watchtower whilst the other guardsmen was speaking to a wagon driver. Ranic turned as he heard someone approaching from behind and rolled his eyes. His skin hadn't improved and even now he was scratching away at one of his scabs. Thalkin fought the urge to empty his stomach at the sight.

'Orphan,' Ranic said acknowledging Thalkin, but then turned back to face the wagon whose driver was now arguing with the other guardsmen, while his wife and two children sat watching the back and forth.

'Ranic, may I have a word?'

'I don't have time can you not see?'

'If you listen to me, I can have you out of this gate patrol.' Thalkin replied, whispering so as not to be overheard.

Ranic's head snapped toward Thalkin, his eyes narrowing. 'What do you mean?'

'I have information that can get you in good stead with the new Commander of the Watch.'

Ranic grabbed Thalkin by the scruff of his shirt and pulled him into the guard tower. He threw him up the ladder. Thalkin climbed to the top, as the other guardsmen lazily looked down. Thalkin noticed his bow was unstrung. The wind was forceful at the top but you could see the southern road that lead to Vadir and Veil. The road split near the base of the great impassable mountains of Veil, with one path leading West to Vadir and the other going through the great defensible Elway Pass, which had stopped the onslaught of the advance of man into Elvish territory. The land to the south was less vegetated than the north due to the strong winds. Although there were copses of trees, which were small and bent to the winds, most of the land was grass with varying sizes of boulders sprayed across it. The mountains of the Veil were monstrous. Even in the moonlight, Thalkin could see the snow-tipped peaks and steep sides. They were a natural defensive wall and one of the reasons why there were any elves left, not counting the sand elves to the west, of course.

'Jannon needs your help down there. I need to teach this one some respect, but can't do it in front of the new citizens of Scor.'

The other guardsmen shrugged, left his unstrung bow and climbed down the ladder. Ranic looked down to make sure he was out of earshot and rounded on Thalkin.

'Now what cow dung of a story have you come up with this time?' He was not scratching now, so Thalkin knew, despite his words, that Ranic was interested in what he had to say.

'It is not a story, if you would be quiet for a few moments I can tell you.'

'Don't make me smack you, thief.' He grabbed Thalkin by the hair.

Thalkin fought against it, but Ranic was too strong. 'You can smack me all you want, pox face, but if you do, I won't tell you what I am more than happy to share with you now.'

He stared at Thalkin for a few moments, then let him go. 'For the sake of Scor, out with it already. I cannot believe I am listening to this.'

'Not yet, I need your oath that you will return the favour.'

Ranic looked ready to explode, his hand hovered over his dirk. Thalkin saw the look in his eyes and believed he would do it. He needed to approach this differently. 'Listen, Ranic. I am not jesting, what I am about to tell you is for the benefit of the town. There is trouble brewing that I have discovered, and if it is not rooted out, it could spell disaster for Scor. If one man could stop it before it had time to grasp hold of the people of this town, then I am positive he would be rewarded. Yet I will not give up this nugget of information for free, so you must return this information with a favour...or two. You know me, Ranic. I do not break my oath.'

Ranic looked him up and down, his anger subsiding. His hand moved away from his weapons and he stood at ease. 'OK Thalkin, you have my word, I will return the favour you give me.' He smiled. 'So, tell me, what will Commander Billan reward me for knowing?'

Thalkin nodded and laid out to him what he knew of Pickfill, his hunters and Breath. 'Pickfill most likely would have left by now but if you round up his hunters, then when he marches into town with the Breath, you will have stopped any chance of this despicable concoction from infecting Scor.'

Ranic was leaning on one of the parapets and let out a breath, the wind whipping at his scruffy hair. He took the whole story in before saying 'That is quite the tale.'

Thalkin raised his hands to the sky. 'It is no tale, I am telling you.'

Ranic waved away Thalkin's exasperated comments. 'I believe you, orphan. You are right, if I were to present this information to Billan and help apprehend these men, I would no longer be standing on this tower or checking under merchants' skirts.' He had a faraway look in his eyes, grinning an ugly grin. Thalkin cleared his throat and Ranic came back from his thoughts. 'OK so I am a man of my word. What would you want in exchange?'

Thalkin tried to hide a smile. 'A merchant who has recently came to town, he needs Pickfill's spot in the market.'

'His name?'

'Momo of Kytosh.'

Ranic nodded. 'I think I know the man, there are not many people here from Kytosh at the moment. I'll make sure he gets the spot. Anything else? Surely you did not put yourself at such great risk for something so small. If they caught you, they would have used you as live bait in the woods'

Thalkin thought for a moment. 'I may need your help in the future, I shall hold you to your oath.'

Ranic did not look pleased. 'I do not like being in someone's debt. Call your favour now or be done with it.'

'It shall not be too great, do not worry but I have no need of your help beyond Momo's claiming of the spot. You know how much this information is worth, you shall be in great stead with Billan. Surely an orphan's desires won't be too great an ask for you.'

Ranic shook his head. 'Have it your way, but if I deem the request to be too great, I shall not go through with it.'

Thalkin did not like the sound of that too much but the chance of not ending up in the town halls dungeon after getting caught surely will not be a great ask of Ranic. He extended his arm and Ranic gripped his forearm.

'Now be off with you, Thalkin. I believe I have some very important errands to run now.' He then turned his back and leant on the parapets looking out into the distance. There was light on the horizon, the false dawn, a dark spot amongst the background. The Black Moon was rising. Thalkin's stomach dropped. Sal would be rising soon. He clambered down the ladder and set off at a run towards Sal and Rosalind's house. He didn't pause for breath even though he was extremely tired. His legs started to burn and in between taking great lungs' full of air, he regularly broke into a yawn. He couldn't stop, he had made a promise to Rosalind and Sal. They'd definitely be upset and disappointed in him. They would probably start treating him like every other family he had been loaned to. He had been fed too well for too long. It was about time he stopped sleeping in a warm bed and started to get used to coming home and defending an angry blow from a drunk father or a spiteful son. He had become complacent. Thalkin was glad they would be angry, as it meant they would show their true self, like everyone else. Let them curse him, slap him and throw him out. It would just mean his normal life had resumed, scraping together some coin to feed himself, stealing, and doing the work he was born to do. He thought about the fighter he had met at Edgir's earlier, Edelia wasn't it? They'd said they had a favour to ask. He was too wrapped up in his current quest to take any notice. Well if his current 'family' wanted to treat him like dirt then he'd happily take Edelia up on her quest. That didn't stop him from running though and before too long he found himself on the street that he had been living on for the past tennight.

He approached the door, and as he raised his hand to grab the door handle, it opened up and Sal towered over him. His face was as passive as usual but there were dark rings below his eyes and when he saw Thalkin, something unusual swept over his face. One of his massive hands grabbed Thalkin's cloak and pulled him into the house. He was carried into the kitchen, his feet barely touching the floor. A few details came to Thalkin's mind. The usual smell of cooked eggs, sausages, cakes, and oats was lacking. Thalkin kept flinching as Sal's hand swung by his side as the mason worker walked, mistaking it for a swing at his head. He was thrown into a chair at the kitchen table, which was empty except for Rosalind who had her head in her hands. Sal walked to the window that looked out into the garden, showing his back to Thalkin. As the boy landed onto the chair, Rosalind's head snapped up.

'Where have you been, Thalkin?' Her eyes were red and her voice broken when she spoke.

The boy didn't answer, he just folded his arms and looked away.

'Answer me!' She slapped the table, making Thalkin jump.

'I was out,' he mumbled.

'Out? We are your carers, Thalkin. If you were hurt under our care---'

'No one would notice. Why should you?' Thalkin snarled.

Rosalind looked offended, he noticed now that she too had dark circles under her eyes. The two had not been to bed yet. 'You think we take this lightly? I do not know why this city takes pride on ignoring their duty but where we are from, we do not casually throw aside those that need help. You know this, I have told you.'

'But we are not where you are from. We are in Scor. It's best you start behaving like it,' Thalkin said his eyes meeting Rosalind's. There was a deep sadness in there.

'Sorry to disappoint you, Thalkin, but we shall do things our way. You made a promise to me, to Sal and you broke that promise.'

'Well kick me out then!' Thalkin stood up, his fury billowing out from nowhere.

'You think it's that easy? We would just hit you and that's it, throw you out? We have done too much for you to throw it away. No, you will wish that we had kicked you out after we are finished with you.' Rosalind was standing too. Her red hair was tied up, but a few strands licked with grey were hanging down, framing her face.

'Oh, I haven't heard that before,' Thalkin said petulantly

Sal turned. 'You think beating is the only punishment we can devise. We are from Renlac, where the people are much smarter than the citizens of Tyton. Like Rosalind said, you'll wish that we'd kicked you out and beaten you.'

'Why do you even care? What is it? You think making me some food, helping you on a building site and giving me a bed somehow makes me yours. Well, I'm not, I am Thalkin of Scor. I was left abandoned when I was a babe and I'm abandoned now. Fifteen years I have been alone and alone is how I shall live. Why don't you have your own kids, if you want one so badly?!'

He knew immediately that he had said something wrong. Rosalind recoiled visibly. Her countenance changed from anger and worry to utter sadness, and she gave him a bleak look of loss. Her eyes welled up and she covered her mouth. Sal came to her side but she pushed him off and ran into the garden, out of sight. Sal's head dropped, his big shoulders shuddering with silent sobs. Thalkin was motionless, his hand rested on the back of the wooden chair and he became very aware of how it felt, the course of the wood, the splintering on its edges and the run of the grain. His anger had totally subsided now and all that was left was deep unyielding guilt.

'We fled Renlac, Thalkin. Me and Rosalind, my amazing, beautiful wife. It was not war, nor famine nor poverty that we ran from but ourselves.' There was a moment of silence as the big man let these words flow out, it was the most expressive that Sal had been. 'We cannot bear our own children. We have tried many times, but the happiest day of a man and woman's life, becomes our worst nightmare. After our third try, we knew it was not to be our destiny. Our town bore too many memories, so we decided to start afresh and found Scor. And you.' Sal looked up and his eyes were red. The tears had stopped, but their marks streaked his face.

The two were silent for a few moments. Thalkin moved forward and placed his hand on Sal's shoulder. 'I am so sorry, Sal. You two have been great to me. I have ruined it.'

Sal nodded and a small smile crept onto his face. 'Nothing is ruined that cannot be amended.' He coughed and squeezed Thalkin's shoulder tenderly for a moment before giving him a big slap. He coughed and straightened up. 'I am late.' He turned to the sink and splashed some water on his face from the bucket. 'Speak to Rosalind, please. We shall talk of your punishment later.' Sal lingered a while, looking at Thalkin, then gazed through the window into the garden, smiling a sad smile and left.

Thalkin took a deep breath, he wiped away the tears that had been building and made his way out into the garden. Rosalind was kneeling at the far side digging and planting. As he approached, he could hear the intermittent in-takes of breaths of someone who was crying. He knelt beside her, as she made a mess of some seed pods, digging erratically, shoving them into the ground. Rosalind stopped when she felt his presence next to her. He slowly began repairing the damage that she had made, gently fixing the pods that would grow into leeks and patted down the uneven soil.

'I promise, never again,' Thalkin said. He was surprised at how his voice broke when he spoke these words.

Rosalind wiped her nose with her wrist. She turned and smiled at Thalkin then shook her head. 'It was wrong for us to make you promise this, you are almost a man now and we treated you like a child. We just want you to know, there is a safe place here for you. The only thing I ask is you take care of yourself.'

He was struck deeply at this moment by the couple's kindness. It was so overwhelming so different to what he was used to, and he realised he had hurt them. 'I shouldn't have said those things, I had no idea.'

Rosalind said nothing, but just bowed her head. 'The Father Sun and Black Moon gives life, Thalkin, but also destroys it. It is the way of our world. The elves are gifted eternal life yet they are blinded by their arrogance and cruelty. We are gifted with the good.' She took Thalkin's hand 'and the bad'. She placed her other hand on her stomach.

Thalkin nodded, gazing up at the Black Moon, which gave off the light from the Father sun, but retained none for itself. 'I shall do my best to live under your rules while I am here.'

Rosalind pulled a face. 'While you are here? Thalkin, I don't think you'll be going anywhere else.
Did Sal not tell you?'

Thalkin shrugged.

'You are to be taken on as an apprentice. He has spoken to his foreman, you were meant to
start today but, well…' She spread her hands out in front of her and shrugged.

'But…I am unsure. Why?'

'Well, he said you had been a good worker over the last few days and you have no particular skill due to your upbringing, so why not? We would have to build you up though.' Once again Rosalind's face was full of pity as she looked him up and down. Thalkin's small malnourished frame had certainly grown a little thanks to his new diet but it was still far from what it should be. Thalkin shuffled nervously. Rosalind was aware of this and looked away. She stood up suddenly and took a deep breath, rubbing her hands on her apron. 'OK first things first, you finish up here and I shall start on your breakfast then you can get some rest. I am assuming you will be starting tomorrow.' She made her way back into the house.

'But Rosalind, what if I fail, what if I shame Sal? I am not too sure about this.'

Rosalind smiled. 'Thalkin, to be fair, it is your only option at this moment.'

Thalkin continued to help Rosalind around the garden until they were both too tired to work any further and retired to their rooms. Thalkin was exhausted both physically and mentally. Sleep was hard to come by, as his mind raced with so much to think on. It was true what Rosalind said, there was not another way for him to build a life for himself. He had been gifted a family who actually cared for him and the chance to become more than just an orphan of Scor. He had hurt Rosalind and Sal unknowingly but still felt deeply guilty about it. Maybe fitting into their lives a bit would help to make up for that. He felt slightly sick to think he would be helping Scor to grow but he could always engrave his name or a crude image in some nook and cranny of a nobleman's home. Maybe he would work one day in Gregori's house and carve an image below his bed of Farmer Thomil's son with little or no manhood. Thalkin smiled at that. Maybe the life of a mason could be fun? With these thoughts in mind, Thalkin finally drifted off to sleep.

Around him was a world of grey. He looked down at his feet and they stood on nothingness. He tried to take a step forward, but nothing happened. There was no air, breeze, or feeling; everything was devoid of sensation. As there was nothing, there was no feeling so there was no panic. Calmly, he thought about what he needed to do. First, he thought, he needed the floor. Then there was a floor. It stretched for a few yards in a square around him. The floor was grey as were the walls, but it was lighter so he could see it. He decided to sit down because now he could, cross-legged. He decided he didn't want to be surrounded by grey so he thought of walls. They were the same colour as the floor and rose to just over his head. He didn't want the ceiling to be like his walls and floor because then it would just be the same as the grey nothing, so he left it as it was to remind him. Now he had a square room but it was only a different shade so he changed the grey wall brown and the floor green, which reminded him of something and made him feel safe. He stood up and walked around his room. It was blank and he wanted to fill it. For the next few minutes, he started to play with his world. He had acquired scope in the grey nothing and so was able to manipulate his surroundings. He looked around and saw his chair and small side table. He turned the ground into grass and the walls into bushes, then created a gentle breeze and the grass gave off a fresh aroma. He turned the square into a rectangle and split it in half with a stream passing through. Small rocks lined the side and the water was so pure you could see the rocks beneath the water, as if liquid glass was passing over them. He could step over the stream but created a small bridge in the middle. He sat down on his chair and leant on the table. He felt tired, fatigued in his bones. Strange. He needed to sleep so he lay down in the grass, feeling it's sponginess and took deep breaths, taking the smell deep into his lungs. As sleep overtook him, he could hear two voices whisper. They were voices familiar but he couldn't place them. He couldn't make out their words and the more he concentrated, the more his fatigue grew and then there was nothingness.

Thalkin woke from a deep, dreamless sleep.

Chapter Five

Thalkin screamed in pain. The hammer had completely missed the nail and bounced off his thumb. He clutched his wrist, trying vainly to stem the pain but he could already feel it swelling. He looked down from the three-storey building he was sitting on and saw the hammer clatter onto the floor, nearly missing another mason. Curses were aimed towards him but Thalkin was more concerned with his thumb. He had already broken the little finger on his left hand and ripped a nail off the right middle finger when it got trapped in a support beam.

'Sal!' Thalkin called over to his friend and master, who was focused firmly on finishing up a wall in what would be a storage building on the south-side of Scor. Sal looked up, however, and nodded. 'Is it OK if I take a few minutes, I dropped my hammer.' Sal looked slightly disappointed, but smiled and turned back to his work.

Thalkin walked towards the scaffolding and before making his descent down, he looked off to the west to the ancient fortress of Scor. He sighed and climbed down. He found his hammer next to some sniggering stone masons but ignored their looks. They would never lay a finger on him like they used to but it didn't stop them from making their comments when Sal wasn't around. To be fair, they had every right to their views. He had been Sal's apprentice for six months but it was becoming apparent that being a stonemason wasn't Thalkin's call in life. Things could have been worse, of course. He was actually getting some coin for doing honest work, he had a home, and Sal and Rosalind Latal were more or less his foster family. He still wistfully thought of Edgir and all the other people who bestowed the odd job on him. He'd had many adventures and would spend night after night reminiscing about them in his bed as the cool summer's air hung lazily around him. Yet his last foray had to be his crowning quest. Pickfill's men had been arrested the moment they had started setting up the stall, and it was handed over to Momo the next day. Then, two days later, Pickfill rode into town and was detained at the border town of Scor with his supply of Breath. Ranic was promoted to Watchman of the city guard and Commander Billian's secretary, and had already proven himself capable in the role, in fact. Thalkin hadn't let Ranic forget that he still owed him a favour though. Momo had been selling his wares, which to Thalkin's surprise were revealed to be books. They were a scarce commodity in Scor, as it was mainly a farming town. There wasn't a single university or library, unlike the great cities of the world, just the town's scholar's personal collection of tomes and reams of parchment. This was where Thalkin had learnt to read and was the main source of literature. Yet people were becoming wealthy and had the time and coin to spend on less essential items. As promised, Momo gave Thalkin some of his wares. Two, to be precise, and Thalkin cherished them. Both were written about the history of Duria, one specifically on the great Kalai, a warrior general who stopped the Schism from consuming the North. He was greatly respected on both sides after stopping an immense force with few soldiers in the Battle of Northern Storms and brokering peace afterwards. He had read it several times and gave as much thought to daydreaming about being a man like Kalai as he did to remembering his own personal triumphs. The next was a deep and complex text about the histories of the world. It was ancient and Thalkin had difficulty reading parts of the text. It was not written in a language that Thalkin could readily translate. In fact, it seemed to be a mix of all the languages of men, the six states of Boras and Novu-Optu. Thalkin could pick out some words and catch the meaning of some sentences but it mainly passed him by. And yet, it was filled with magnificent sketchings, showing the ancient world, people, cities and buildings that had long since decayed and fallen into ruin most likely. That was why Thalkin persevered with it; he needed to understand it and find out the book's secrets. The knowledge that lay within the book would most likely have no use for the former urchin, yet he could not help but have a hunger to know more. It had no name and had a plan non-descript cover but Thalkin had come to calling it the History of Duria.

Momo said he had no use of them since most people did not want to read about the past, but of the future instead. Wives who stayed at home wanted to read about the great tales of romance, and their husbands were more than obliging to pay for reasons that were beyond Thalkin. Momo was leaving Scor today, in fact, after 6 months he had exhausted his entire stock and had made arrangements to collect his next batch of literature at Freedom's Pass in Tyton. Thalkin, dusting off his hammer, decided that now would be the perfect time to say goodbye and so set off for the Flayed Dragon's Inn, where Momo had set up his temporary home.

The rumour had come true and official word finally came through to Lord Thomil of the decision that Scor was not only to become a city but also a Borasian state that was completely independent of Tyton. As a result a day of celebration was held. Only a few traders worked, Momo included as he only held the stand for two days and the announcement was apparently part of his plan. Lord Thomil stood atop the fountain, like the preacher had, and proclaimed that Scor was now free. Every man and woman who helped and continued to help Scor grow into a great Borasian state would reap the benefits. He thanked them and gave all his workers the day off, which meant half the city and the other half followed suit. Thalkin was standing shoulder to shoulder with his permanent carers and could not help but smile and revel in their happiness. Seeing Sal cheer was a shock which brought laughter to Thalkin, genuine warm laughter. They all got drunk, along with the whole town, and gorged on cakes, pies and various other delicacies. Lord Thomil proclaimed it would be a true Borasian state and that he would, despite his family having made the town what it was, 'Pass on the flame to guide Scor into the future, to the next Lord Procterate.' Thalkin couldn't help but scoff even though everyone cheered. Young as Thalkin was, who had now seen sixteen summers, he knew that Thomil would never lose his power over Scor. The Law of the Borasian States dictated that only a man who held claim to a business could decide on the next Lord Procterate. Since Thomil owned almost half of Scor he was guaranteed to remain the Lord Procterate for a long time, which also meant Gregori. Thalkin saw him, smiling cockily at the crowds gathered as if he already owned them. He caught Thalkin's stare and his smile turned into a snarl.

Six months on from that night Scor had truly exploded. A palisade was being built far beyond the city's border, for at least a mile, and a true stone wall was set to be built around the city proper. The palisade was designed to keep the closest farms protected as well as to quickly set up as many gates and entrances as possible so that Thomil could claim a tax from merchants who entered the city. Thalkin had helped build it. The workforce was huge and the provisional city wall was up and running in no time. Work had not yet started on the stone wall, but it was not far off from starting. Homes, warehouses and places of industry were all being constructed. Thalkin could only guess their purposes of most of them, such as granaries, lumber yards, and sewers to clean the city's water supply. Thalkin noticed a few of the larger buildings being fitted for what seemed to be smithying. What intrigued Thalkin about this however was that a smithy was generally big enough for only one or two workers, yet these buildings were being set up to allow five to ten workers inside. The pillared building that Thalkin wondered about was to be a large temple dedicated to the new religion spreading through the land. Most people worshipped at the shrines either in their homes or around the town. Over the past two centuries fewer and fewer Southerners followed The Word, the dogma of the North and instead started listening more to the Old Gods, legends and myths whose full stories had been lost to antiquity. For this reason, there was a spiritual void in most people's lives and the Temple of Self began to fill that void. The religion of the mystical elves spoke of a God within every living thing and taught that peace among the many started with peace within oneself. Now that the building was finished a 'teacher' would help people to find this inner peace. Thalkin did not bother and could always find a better use of his time then sitting in a room breathing.

Thalkin walked among these new buildings that were springing into life until he reached the town centre, where he found Momo almost immediately. He was laughing and joking with a hired hand to help him prepare for his journey. To Momo's delight, his entire stock had been bought and since his books were not cheap, he had made quite a profit from his time in Scor. He had enjoyed the gold that he had earned, which was evident by his new robes. These were black with a gold trim and his fingers were covered with silver rings. His wagon was being pulled by a strong shire horse and a hired sword sat atop it, sharpening a nasty looking bastard sword. His red hair was braided like a warrior, as well as his fiery red beard. Thalkin took stock of the hidden daggers, and the short axe that sat at his right side. Scars dotted the skin that was not covered by his travelling armour. An experienced fighter did not come cheap.

'Thalkin!' Momo boomed and shuffled over to Thalkin. 'My savvy friend, how are you?'

It was a near impossibility to not smile when Momo greeted him. Thalkin was starting to feel a rich man with the friends he was gathering. It was why he was going to miss Momo while he was gone. During the past six months, no matter how busy Momo was at his stall, he always had time for Thalkin. It was a strange feeling to be wanted. 'Momo, I am good, tired but good.'

'Masonry work suits you. You have grown already, the tiredness is a sign of your growth.' He slapped Thalkin on the shoulder, who winced. Momo was right. He had definitely started to fill out. Being fed steady and hearty meals mixed with a physical craft was good for his strength and fitness, even though he was tired and sore almost all the time.

'You are not wrong. So, almost ready to begin your journey?'

'Yes, almost, I am dropping some goods off to my friend, who is meeting me at Freedom's Pass. He is thinking of setting up shop at Scor and wants to see the competition.'

'How long will you be gone for?' Thalkin prayed it wasn't too long

Momo's eyes looked up as he thought. 'It would be a month. We plan to hit Freedom's Pass in just under a tennight.' He turned to look at his hired sword, who slowly nodded his approval. 'Meet up with my friend then journey back to Traveller's Inn, where we will celebrate our success and talk business. Then head back with a wagon full of goods.'

'Books?'

'And more my friend, and more.' Momo's grin revealed his yellow teeth and he rubbed his hands together, a typical gesture from Momo whenever he got excited about money.

Thalkin nodded and smiled at this friend's enthusiasm. 'Traveller's Inn? I have not heard of this.'

Momo's mouth dropped open but shut quickly again with understanding. 'I would be shocked but I realise not everyone is a merchant. Travelers Inn is a place where all the business in the world is discussed.' He knelt and drew a map in the earth. 'You have Tyton here, it connects the North, South and West. The sea brings trade from the North, due to the water next to Vadir, which flows South, the cheapest and sometimes quickest way is to go through Tyton. It is the same with Gorshondrax and even the Veil, when those bastard Elves decide to not be arrogant whoresons. This means that Tyton connects them all. The corridor to Renlac, Freedom's Pass, connects the rest of the world. The only road that brings it all together is Fyn's Road.' Thalkin watched quietly, he even noticed that the warrior and labourer had stopped what they were doing and were looking interested in what Momo was saying. 'Between all this movement, all this money, Thalkin, is Traveller's Inn.' He looked up beaming, Thalkin realised he'd never had a conversation with Momo that didn't include a smile from the Kytoshian man.

'I am missing something, it's just an Inn.'

Momo mocked exasperation, 'It is because you have not seen it, inn does not do it justice, I admit. It is more of a keep. A huge three-storey beehive, filled with the people who move all the gold in the world. If it is going to be sold or bought, then it can be found in Travelers Inn.'

Thalkin nodded, understanding more as to why Tyton was the richest state in Boras.

Momo rubbed his dirtied hands against his robes and stood up. 'I believe I am almost ready and must be off my friend.' He made a gesture to the labourer to hurry up, who ran to grab the last of Momo's belongings.

'I see why you need the extra hand.' Thalkin nodded to the warrior who had returned to checking his gear.

'Well, not only that. Tyton unfortunately, is a wild country. The Green Wilds have some vicious creatures that are known to attack caravans so a single caravan would be tempting to them.'

'Neckaleeves, kill one and three grow from its body. Foul ugly creatures that carry disease wherever they go,' Thalkin said nodding.

'Aye, boy you have heard of them, but you do not know the full truth.' The warriors growling voice came like a sudden thunder-storm. 'Their very bodies are decaying. Their top half is a man with blackened sagging skin, and their bodies are mottled with grey fur that irritates the skin. Their legs, as weak as they look, can chase down a man on flat land, even over the rocky, desolate Green Wilds they can keep up. When you slay them, their kind will lay their eggs on the dying body and when their weak offspring hatches they feast off their dead kin. Only way to fully destroy them, is to burn them. If you fight them, you make sure you burn your clothes.'

Thalkin shuddered and Momo didn't look like his usual cheerful self, but then he suddenly burst out laughing. 'Thalkin, if you ever decide to become a sellsword, this is how you do business!' He shook his head as he climbed on the wagon.

'Well, a stonemason is my life now.' He let his disappointment show in his voice, dropping his guard just for a moment, and Momo picked it up.

'This town does not deserve you. Be well Thalkin, I shall see you soon.' Momo nodded to the warrior who then whipped the reigns on the horse and they moved away, making their way north. It seemed that the Latals would be his only company for the next few tennights, but he could do a lot worse.

Thalkin walked to the top of the hill and watched the wagon roll down the North Road. It was overcast and Thalkin could smell the rain in the air. He had to go back to the work-site, but looking at the hills and forests, and the lands to the north, he didn't want to move. There were also the mountains to the west with the old stronghold which was talked about in his old book. It spoke of a mountain embedded in the rock. Thalkin was certain other keeps were built into mountains across the world, but there was a familiarity about the words. Thalkin spoke the Tyton dialect, of course, and could understand and hold a conversation with someone from Vadir, and he was now learning Renlac with some speed. Gorshandrax and Kalak were his weak points. He could get by as he spoke the trader's tongue that was known simply as Borasian but having a complete understanding was a distant target and the tongue of Novu-Optu was completely unknown to him. There was a magic in how the stronghold in the text was discussed. Something ancient and divine was held in there. It wasn't smart to keep on assuming that the stronghold in the book was the one he was looking at now. He knew it was childish to daydream and hope that he was so close to something written about in the book he was reading. Yet, for some reason, he could not help but imagine that the Scor stronghold just so happened to be the place discussed in the book. The history of Duria spoke of a mountainous stronghold that *'buried darkness to stop it from reaching the sky'*. It filled him with curiosity so that at any given moment he found himself staring off at the stronghold. The strong, thick base that slanted upwards would make it hard for anyone to scale the wall, as ladders would simply slide off. As the base was further away from the top of the wall, grappling hooks would have to be thrown inwards and not just upwards. Thalkin had not seen any other castles, he had asked traders and people who came from outside of Scor and they confirmed any castles, keeps or fortresses were not of the same design. It was too difficult to build as the stress on the wall reaching backwards would cause it to topple. Mostly the walls were vertical with walkways at the top jutting out slightly. The infamous Lasting Keep and Creeping Fort, two of the greatest castles in all of Duria could not boast walls such as this and the people of Kalak and Moosh were masters of defensive engineering. Building into the rock face must help with this but there was something else, even from distance Thalkin could sense something was different.

He sighed as he brought himself out of his daydream. He was behind on his work and had already taken up too much time today. He wound his way through the mud-packed streets and cobbled roads, where people were still going about their day, as the rush of city life had certainly descended upon Scor. The streets were getting too crowded as he made his way through the market district as it was now called. The city had been growing since Thalkin had been a pup, constantly working to become more than just a bane of Tyton. There had been some rough winters as Thomil pushed the city to its limits by selling off large amounts of produce so that he could put the money back into the town for greater growth. To be truthful, Thalkin barely survived. He remembered one winter in which he had been close to death and it was then that he became acquainted with Edgir. He was fed and sheltered for only a week before he had to steal a keg of ale for the former rival of Thomil. Edgir had used Thalkin and would threaten him; if he did not go out and commit his petty crimes he would not be fed. Thalkin could not disagree that he was earning his keep and learning the secrets of the city, and he helped the former brawler turned businessman gain a handsome sum in a bribe after discovering the owner of the Flayed Dragon visited a travelling bard whilst his wife was asleep.

Thalkin turned down a narrow alley to avoid the bustle, which was slowing him down, and saw his building site poke its unfinished head over the next row of houses opposite him. He took a moment, taking in the unique quietness of the street. His guard was down so he did not hear the footsteps behind him and reacted way too late when a hand grasped his throat. After being slammed into the wall, he instinctively grabbed the hand that tried to choke him. A few punches landed on his body, and he put his guard low, but the strikes were then aimed at his head. He ignored them as best he could and twisted the hand that grabbed him. His attacker's body naturally followed where he pulled forcing his guard down. Thalkin stepped forward and struck down with his elbow towards the face of his target, he felt his elbow connect with a skull and launched himself forward with his knee. He heard a cough as his knee winded someone. He had a moment to take in his attacker, correction - attackers. Gregori, Jon, and Dill, of course.

They stood before him, spread out along the alleyway; it was already narrow but now there was no way past except through Gregori.

'You've grown, Thalkin.' Gregori had hate in his eyes.

'As have you.' And he had. Thalkin heard that Gregori had taken a hands-on role within his father's farm, learning the business from the lowest level of his future legacy. He would inherit the lands and most likely the title of Lord Procterate. To do that successfully he needed to understand what his workers experienced so that he would know how best to gain their support. Just like Thalkin, he found the hard days of toil had added pounds of muscle; boyhood was certainly behind the two rivals. However, Gregori was still the bigger of the two, as he had always been. It wasn't the only thing he noticed though. Down by Gregori's hip was a very real and dangerous looking sword. They all had them, sheathed for now. 'Still ugly though, farm boy.'

Gregori's fists clenched. 'I never got to thank you for beating me and my friends. You were very disappointed in Thalkin, weren't you Jon?'

Jon simply cracked his necked.

'And poor Dill, I'm sure you had a few words to say.'

'More than his father probably said to his mother.' Dill, the stumpy lackey, sneered.

Thalkin's teeth started to grind. He tried to remember the promise he had made to Sal and Rosalind but his mind was now becoming hazy.

'I've started to work with Thalkin's mother on the farm you know, Dill. The mare's in heat, almost ready to be mounted by the stallion.' Dill and Jon started to snicker, as Gregori began to make more references to Thalkin's unknown mother and the farm animals he now worked with.

'Please, I just want to get to work.' Thalkin looked over his shoulder but the distance to the street was too great, they would catch up with him. He needed to get through, plus running away didn't sit well with Thalkin.

'Listen, you pox son of a whore. You are lucky my father hasn't had you strung up. You are a leech on this city, if it wasn't for that pretty bitch and stone head you live with---'

The sound of Thalkin's fist on Gregori's jaw was like a hammer on stone. The Lordlings head snapped back and Thalkin dove on him, punching and biting. He felt his knuckles hit the soft cartilage of the nose, the sharp edges of teeth and the rounded thick forehead. Something hard struck the back of Thalkin's skull and his vision blurred, his body sagged and nothing responded for a moment. The next thing he was aware of was Jon and Dill kicking his ribs and head. He curled up and tried to roll away but the strong hands of Jon grabbed the back of his tunic and threw him up against the wall. He pushed forward to fight but he heard metal slide along leather and saw, a flash of light. The tip of an iron sword was now an inch from his neck. Gregori's red and partially swollen face was breathing hard, spittle and blood had mixed together to make a stringy mess across the otherwise handsome face. His short blonde hair was dirty and dishevelled as it hung loosely across his eyes.

'We could gut you right now and no one would miss you.' Gregori had the look of a crazed murderer on his face. Dill struck Thalkin across the face, making him spit blood, then Jon slapped him hard, making him stand up to face Gregori again. 'You are a stain on this great city, one that my father has built, and his father. You piss on my legacy.' The sword was drawing closer until Thalkin felt it press against the flesh on his throat. He feared to swallow in case it cut his skin.

'Gregori, that's enough.' Dill said, his voice was full of uncertainty.

There was a burning sensation and then something hot trickled down his neck and into his shirt.

'Gregori, you cut him, stop.' Now the silent oaf decided to open his mouth for once.

Thalkin wasn't going to lie, he was scared. He saw the look in Gregori's eyes, he would kill Thalkin if he knew he could get away with it and he could.

'Just a slice and it'll all be over, orphan. You will be out of everyone's way. I mean what are you going to do with your life? There is nothing for you in Scor, believe me I will make sure of it.' The last sentence came out like a hiss of venom and hate.

Thalkin swallowed, the blade pressed tighter and he felt more blood trickle down. 'Gregori, please…' Gregori smiled at the thought of Thalkin now begging. 'Please take your sword and shove it up your father's criminal arse.'

The blade moved away as Gregori recoiled at the slight. 'I am going to kill you.' Gregori pulled back his blade and aimed low for Thalkin's stomach. Jon and Dill still held Thalkin in place, much to their discomfort. Thalkin's stomach lurched, his bowels turned to water, and he closed his eyes. Yet there was no impact; instead, there was a ring of metal on metal, a grunting of pain and the vice-like grips of Jon and Dill eased up. When he opened his eyes Dill and Jon had their backs to the wall as Gregori retreated backwards, frantically blocking a rapid succession of blows from a sword-wielding warrior with a long grey, braided ponytail.

He fell on his rear end, the sword skittering along the floor. He scrambled backwards as Edelia advanced with her sword pointing at the inheritor of Scor. Terror was etched on his face as he hit the wall and the sword tip was levelled at him. Thalkin saw movement and spotted Dill crawling for the sword behind Edelia. There was a satisfying crunch as Dill's nose made contact with Thalkin's boot, definitely breaking it. The apprentice picked up the sword and pointed it at Dill. He saw Jon Wester lying prone in the background, obviously out cold. The sword was heavy in his hands and the end was visibly shaking. He could see Edelia watching him.

She turned back to Gregori 'I think you've had your fun. You should head home now.'

Gregori looked frightened but there was still that arrogant defiance in his voice. 'Just wait until my father hears of this!'

'Your father will know nothing of this, unless he wants the whole city knowing that his son has pulled a blade on an innocent. I believe the penalty of which is the severing of limbs? I'm not sure, maybe you should ask your father?'

With his hands still raised, he got to his feet and simply shook his head, hatred on his face. 'I want my sword.'

'Oh no, that is mine now. I have defeated you, it is only customary. My advice to you, you should go back to the practice yard before you start walking around with a blade, you are more likely to hurt yourself than anyone else.' Without looking she held out her hand towards Thalkin, who noticed the sword was almost touching the floor, so unused he was to the weapon. He handed it over and shook his arms from fatigue.

Gregori hissed an order and Dill roused Jon, who clumsily got to his feet. They made their way out of the north entrance of the alley whilst Gregori backed out the other. He glared at Thalkin until turning at the very last moment onto the busy street.

Edelia sheathed her blade and began to unclasp her cloak to wrap around the sword.

'Please, allow me.' Thalkin had unclasped his cloak already and offered it to Edelia. She raised an eyebrow but took it anyway, wrapping the weapon with Thalkin's cloak. 'Thank you for saving me.'

She shrugged. 'I am not too keen on unfair fights, although before he drew his sword you were holding your own. Did Edgir teach you to fight like that?'

Thalkin nodded.

'Course, he did, Den Fist I believe he calls it. Well, good morning.' Edelia tipped her head and turned north. Thalkin followed her. 'Is there something else? I will return the cloak.'

'Apologies, my work site is not far from here, it was where I was heading before I was attacked.'

'Ah, a mason. Well that is the perfect job for Scor, no shortage of work.'

'Well, apprentice.' *And a glorified one at that*.

They walked along together for a few moments in silence.

'You have good footwork,' Edelia commented

'Thank you, still all thanks to Edgir.'

'I doubt that, I know he is a great brawler and few can match him in his Den Fist, or so I have been told, but I do not consider him a good teacher. A drunk like that couldn't teach a fish to swim unless it had good instincts.' She turned and looked him up and down. 'Yes, you should take pride in what you have taken from Edgir.'

Thalkin merely grunted, not used to being complimented.

'Do you like the stonework, are you good at it?'

Thalkin shook his head. 'I'm good at lifting things, but the more complex side of the work...' he halted, leaving the rest to go unsaid.

Edelia looked forward. 'Wielding a blade is not too far off fighting with your fists you know. The footwork is almost the same, it requires discipline of the mind and timing. The rest is just getting used to the extra weight and reach.'

'And the fact you are killing someone.'

Edelia smiled. 'Well, that's where blade work has its benefits.' She laughed at her own joke.

Thalkin didn't know how to respond.

Edelia had stopped laughing now. 'Listen, Master Thalkin, I have been in Scor for almost half a year now, but I plan on staying for a few months more. If you would like some lessons, I would be happy to teach you.'

Thalkin was taken aback. Learn to use a sword? He had daydreamed of being the mighty Kalai but did not think an opportunity would present itself. Excitement began to flutter in his belly but then his guard came up. 'What would it cost?'

It was Edelia's turn to look surprised. Lately Thalkin had been good at spotting someone who was masking their true feelings. He'd always had a good read on people but it had developed almost into an extra sense, like the smell of rain in the air, that helped him to detect if there was truth in them. 'Who said I was going to charge?'

'No one ever does anything for free.' Thalkin had stopped now. The street opened up to the left and the work-site was visibly down the lane.

Edelia looked down at Thalkin and a knowing look passed on her face. 'I will ask something of you. My offer stands.' Edelia unclasped her cloak and gave Thalkin's back. 'I have taken up residence as Edgir's neighbour. Meet me there, just after sundown and we shall discuss the arrangements.'

'Maybe.' Thalkin backed away and nodded before turning to head to his work-site.

'Thalkin,' Edelia called after him, and the young man turned around to face her, 'you truly do have the footwork of a swordsman.' With that she marched off.

Thalkin could not concentrate all day. Remarks on his tardiness and the hushed comments that would usually make him throw something went ignored. Even Sal asked if anything was the matter. All the young mason could think about was his two books, but now the name next to the great feats in battle was no longer Kalai, it was Thalkin.

Chapter Six

Thalkin bent his knees slightly and raised his arm once more.

'Nope,' Edelia said and tapped him with the broadside of her sword on the places where his positioning was incorrect. Although it was only a tap, getting hit the with iron still stung, but Thalkin was improving. He lifted his knees up slightly and bent his arm just a fraction. 'Correct. Why do you think this stance is the correct one, Thalkin?'

The apprentice had some idea from his training with Edgir. 'I don't want to present a full target so I stand sideways, my knees are bent so they can react quicker, and my arm is primed to strike or block.'

'Yes.' She walked around him in circles. 'Strike.' Thalkin slid his front foot forward followed by his back left foot and lunged with his sword and then snapped back into position. 'Very good, Thalkin. I can tell you are used to fighting, but your sword arm is showing signs of fatigue. Understandably it is your first lesson, but we must build this up.' Then, in a flash, Edelia struck out with her sheathed sword and Thalkin's weapon came flying out of his hands. Thalkin rubbed his sore wrist and allowed a grimace in Edelia's direction. She gave him a disapproving look.

'Edelia, I have worked all day, I am naturally tired, especially my arms, I have been banging a hammer or holding stone, or wood in place.' Thalkin shook his head at his day's work.

'The person who is trying to kill you will not care and will strike with all their might, Thalkin. Most likely you have been marching all day, carrying your weapons in full battle gear when an ambush happens upon you. A sore and tired wrist will see your head rolling on the ground with your body still standing, before it collapses onto the ground.' Edelia struck Thalkin on the backside to march him along to pick up Gregori's sword. No repercussions had come Edelia's way as she had predicted, but Thalkin knew something would befall him at some point. If it did, he would be ready. He couldn't bear the thought that Gregori would master him at some form of fighting. It was one of the few things he had on the Lord Procterate's son.

It is was why he was determined to make the most of this lesson, it could be the last. So, without complaint he picked up the sword and set his mind to ignore the fatigue that had settled deep in his joints and bones. He got into position straight away and lunged and slashed just as Edelia had shown him. He held the sword with his right hand and his left was raised aloft behind him. His back hand was his balance, like the many animals of prey who used their tail to balance out the sharp turns as they chased down their hunt. Edelia had struck him two more times but the sword remained in Thalkin's hand although it did sway from the power of Edelia's blow. She seemed happy all the same.

They had decided to train in the woods, the setting sun cast rays through the branches, giving them as much light as it could. The meadow they trained in was a small clearing, with a few berry bushes and a large rock in the centre. Edelia sat on it eating some plucked berries as Thalkin trained. There was a young sapling which Thalkin was using as his target, but made a point not cutting or damaging the tree, which Edelia did not comment on. After an hour of the routines of stances, strikes and positions Edelia declared they should have a sparring session.

'Do not worry, Thalkin I shall not be aiming to gut you. I'm surprised I thought you were made of more.'

'That is not it, Edelia,' Thalkin stammered. Training with Edgir he hadn't been afraid to take a strike or two, even at full force. He always thought that, with every strike landed on him, it would only make him tougher. However, with a sword, if one strike lands, he might not get up again. 'I am concerned that my inexperience will lead to my own injury, at your hands or mine.'

'I have been a warrior for 30 years Thalkin, and killed many people, and I've been on the verge of death myself. Have you ever seen an arachnataur? No well, I have slain a few. You could not harm me if my sword was sheathed and my breeches were down. I could shave off that fluff of a beard and you wouldn't feel a tingle the next morning. Now do not insult me any further and raise your guard.'

Edelia whipped out her blade, the hand and a half was several inches larger than Thalkin's single-hand sword. She held hers in a similar fashion to Thalkin's and he could already see the years of experience, the flawlessness of her stance, the steadiness of her blade, and the calculating stare that her eyes were giving Thalkin. He got into stance as best as he could manage and Edelia sprang into action. Thalkin immediately doubled back, but his feet got caught and he tumbled to the ground, cursing as he did so.

Edelia pinched her nose and then said sternly, 'Thalkin, listen to me, your blade is an extension of your arm. You can fight, I have seen you. Do not think this as a new world, think this of an addition to a school that you are already a part of.' She held out her hand and helped him up. Thalkin felt embarrassed. She was right, the footwork was not so different so he should not be making a buffoon of himself. Edelia turned away and got herself into position again while Thalkin took his time. Remembering his training with Edgir calmed his mind, as he thought of only his body and got into position. He nodded to Edelia, confirming he was ready.

Edelia again sprang forward. Birds flocked from the trees and there was a scattering of animals as metal clashed on metal in the opening glade. Edelia advanced forward striking with sideways attacks, which Thalkin blocked, once, twice, three times before moving forward and attacking in the same fashion. There was nothing in the session that Thalkin had not seen on the guard's mustering field. So far he had only learned the stances, standard attacks and defensives so he stuck within what was taught. He felt sluggish at first but put all his concentration into what he was doing. Before long everything in the world became a dim hum and all that existed, was block, block, block, strike, strike, front foot first, followed by back foot, and he felt himself settling into a rhythm. Thalkin's movement was becoming more fluid and efficient. Edelia must have known it too because she began to quicken the pace, setting on Thalkin with sharper strikes, sometimes mixing up her attacks but Thalkin remained focused and blocked each of them with little trouble.

It wasn't long before he was dripping with sweat and his lungs burned with his constant gasping, and Edelia gave him little time for respite. Thalkin would not stop until he was told otherwise. The sword was now becoming a part of him. He was no longer affected by the weight; it almost seemed natural to him now. They must have been going for some time before Edelia decided to really impress upon Thalkin the need to stay focused. After an intentionally sloppy strike to Thalkin's right side, she moved in with her shoulder pushing Thalkin back, and then went forward, intending to stop her sword just short of Thalkin's unguarded neck. She was attempting to drop Thalkin's guard and teach him the lesson of never falling under any rhythm and to always be prepared. However, when her follow-up attack came through, Thalkin was not there, he had rolled to the side and was pushing Edelia in her side. Edelia was a veteran of countless sword fights, skirmishes and brawls though, and when Thalkin went to follow-up with his strike, she was blocking it and they fell into another rhythm. After a few more back and forths, Edelia called a halt on the sparring.

The grey warrior walked to the rock in the middle of the glade, took a long pull from the waterskin and threw it to Thalkin, who was now bent over. It hit him on the shoulder and fell to the floor, as did the apprentice as he was overcome with exhaustion. He picked the waterskin up and drank deeply, spitting some into his cupped hand to wash his face. Thalkin had been taking another few gulps when Edelia came over to him and offered him her hand. Thalkin took it and stood up smiling at Edelia.

'Thank you so very much. I don't think I have ever enjoyed anything as much as that.' His grin was full of satisfaction and joy.

Edelia smiled back with her eyebrows raised. 'Well I am glad.' Her brow then furrowed. 'Thalkin, the move where you sidestepped me after I pushed you, is that something Edgir showed you?'

Thalkin looked up, trying to remember. He shrugged. 'No, I don't think so, you never really roll in a fist-fight from what I've seen. It just felt natural, I thought you were going to come in after me and I was off-balance, so I just went with the momentum and popped up at your side.'

Edelia's face was unreadable and she simply nodded. 'You adapted well, Thalkin. I must say. Now, to discuss your next lesson.' She turned and sat down on the rock and Thalkin followed suit. He handed her the waterskin and she took another mouthful.

'What do you need?' Thalkin asked bluntly. He knew that to get another lesson a trade-off must be made. Edelia had made that quite clear from the beginning.

The old warrior finished off the waterskin and set it aside. 'I trust that anything that is discussed is kept strictly between us?'

Thalkin nodded.

'Good. What do you know of Lord Thomil?'

Thalkin shrugged. 'As much as anyone, he comes from a long line of farmers and owners of this land. His father had a dream of expanding Scor to be more than just a bane to Tyton, and Thomil took up that dream with earnest. He has expanded their production of their famous wine, perry and rum into other areas of agriculture. Nothing I hear suggests it comes close to the men of Dorfinbrine in terms of production but it gives enough sustenance to Scor that food never needs to be bought elsewhere, and any excess can be sold. He has bought up other businesses and owns the lumber mill, which also helps with trade. He has a hand I hear in the smithies, as well as many taverns and inns, helping everywhere he can to grow the business. His most significant contribution was opening trade with the Elves of the Veil. It seemed to boost trade and traffic through the town like never before. That's just what everyone else knows.'

'And what do you know about him?' Edelia's face was typically unreadable. Thalkin could feel her studying and watching him, as if she was trying to see what was being unsaid between his words.

'He's a hard, driven man. Cruel and uncaring at least to me but then so is the rest of the town. He has crushed anyone who has opposed him and driven them out of town or flattened them so they are a shadow of their former selves.'

'Edgir.'

Thalkin nodded. 'He plans to build a larger wall to protect the city proper.' Edelia shifted her weight as Thalkin said this, leaning forward with her hands under her chin. 'With what used to be the stone from the Stronghold of Scor, or at least the mountain around it. We will use it as our quarry and create a truly great city.'

'We?'

'I am a mason now.'

'You are helping to build this city'

'I am.' It was the first time Thalkin had thought of it like this and he was unsure of how he felt. He knew, however, it was difficult to say it out loud. Edelia kept silent, still staring at Thalkin, so he continued. 'He is to rebuild the stronghold. Some masons have been assigned to study it and decide on where it needs improving and rebuilding. It is proving to be difficult, however, as the Elves have the knowledge of the old structures and they do not share secrets.'

'Yet Lord Thomil would have the best chance.' Edelia added.

'It seems that way.'

'And how do you know all this? I was unaware that apprentices would know all this information.'

'The building of the wall is already being prepared, they are finishing some buildings up now and will soon begin the work proper on the city wall. As for the Stronghold itself, well, I am good at listening and people are used to ignoring the small urchin.'

'Small no longer though,' Edelia observed.

'Yes, who knew that hard work and filling food would be so beneficial to an orphan? No one from Scor, I can assure you.'

Edelia smiled. 'Well, fair enough, Thalkin. I think you have given me enough information to warrant a few more lessons. I knew some of these things already but a few I didn't. Asking questions is a good way to get hurt. You can count that as one of your lessons, so having someone who is trustworthy is a considerable help. When will it be good for you to train again?'

Thalkin looked up into the sky and saw the sun was setting and was reminded of something. 'I do not have an answer yet.' Thalkin thought of the promise he had made. He could not break it again and he knew Edelia's request would force him to break that promise.

'Well, apprentice, you know where to find me.' She sheathed her sword and gathered her things up and put them in her pack. Thalkin's sword was lying in the grass where he had collapsed, and she nodded towards it.

'I do not think I can keep that, Edelia. Gregori would never approach you for it, but if he ever saw me with it, it would be another question altogether. I think you should keep hold of it, it is yours after all.'

Edelia nodded her understanding and picked it up, using her cloak to wrap it up like she had the first time. She bade Thalkin a good night and made her way towards the city.

Before she entered the tree line, a thought occurred to Thalkin and he didn't think of stopping himself before asking it. 'Why do you want to know about Thomil, Edelia?'

She stopped and stood there, barely a foot away from the treeline, showing her back to Thalkin. A few moments went by before she turned and repeated, 'Asking questions could get you hurt, apprentice.' Her face betrayed no emotion. She nodded once more and disappeared into the forest.

Thalkin's sweat had soaked his clothes and he was beginning to cool down. So it wasn't surprising that he shivered, but it may not have been down to the dampness of his tunic.

Chapter Seven

Thalkin leaned back, trying to crack his back as it burned in agony. He felt like he had been digging for hours. It was late summer so a cold night was not uncommon, but it was blistering hot today and the work was fatiguing. Up and down men were digging a 12-foot wide, 6-foot deep trench that would work as the foundations of the city walls. He was knee-deep in dirt and had been for the past few days. His body still ached from the training he had undergone with Edelia; muscles that he didn't know existed stretched and screamed as he slammed his spade into the cool earth. A repetitive slap and grunt echoed to his left and right as his colleagues pushed on in the heat. The foreman paced up and down, giving encouragement and water to the men, who were on the verge of collapse. Thalkin was impressed by the fervour and determination that Thomil could spread in his people.

The day after Thalkin's training, they had finished the building they were working on and Thomil had gathered all the tradesman and workers together in the town square. He stood atop the fountain, just like he did when he announced that Scor was to be a city, and declared how proud he was of them and inspiring the work had been.

'Scor is built not by my family, but by your bloody hands and sweat on your brows. Some may say that's why it smells!' This caused a few laughs and Thomil let them die down, while his long black leather coat with dire-panther's fur flapped in the cool evening wind. 'But no, I say your hands have created such solid foundations that Scor will never stumble, never teeter, but stand steadfast instead in the coming times. That is why tomorrow we begin work on the most ambitious project the South has ever seen. We shall no longer think of Scor Keep as just a relic from our Elvish overlords past, but reclaim it for the Men of Boras! It shall be Scor's Keep for today and tomorrow!' Even Sal was smiling as the people around him cheered. 'A city wall built from the stone that surrounds us; white and shining like a beacon that will show how Scor is no longer a footnote on a mighty state, but a mighty state itself. In a moon's time, the leaders of Boras will be coming to our state and seeing for themselves that they were not wrong to give the Lord Procterate to you.' He spread out his arms inviting them all in. His eyes were wide and manic, and his barrel chest was heaving in and out. He dropped his hands and knelt down on one knee and all leant in to hear his words. 'We will dig deep into the ground and begin the foundations, bringing the stone and rubble that our fine stonemasons will use to erect the giant wall that will surround our city and protect it from our envious enemies.' He stood up now. 'Make no mistake, we will have enemies, they will covet our riches and new wealth and only with this wall will we be able to stop them. You are the first line, you are the heroes, you are men of Scor!'

A cheer rose up that had never been heard in Scor before. A war cry of hundreds of tired workers who had found a new energy and strength after a long day's work. Thalkin could not help but feel goosebumps. If it hadn't been for his searing rage he felt toward Gregori and the knowledge that Thomil was a lying manipulator, he would have been swept up in it too. He had not thought Thalkin was a part of Scor when he'd cast him aside to make this city. Now that he needed extra bodies, he didn't care who worked on the wall. Thalkin heard Sal's grunting next to him as he mindlessly dug. The huge, caring man who Thalkin now considered a friend was caught up in the fervour too, just like every man who worked next to him. Thomil's speech did the job, and more and more workers were pouring into the city. Thalkin wasn't sure where the coin was coming from, but Thomil had it to spend and he spent it on work hands. From the first day the army of workers went from a few hundred to nearly a thousand, all working from sunrise to sunset. Shifts were not really a concept anymore; men would, instead, work until they collapsed. They would then be helped by their comrades, carried to makeshift tents, and nursed back to strength before going straight back to the trench. After a few hours the stonemasons would get out and walk down the line to a completed section of the trench and begin constructing the foundation. They would create a frame with wood, then place large stones, followed by rubble, around the side and cover it with lime mortar. Each stone was carefully crafted after it was delivered by the quarry at Scor's Keep. Thalkin had not yet seen the quarry, but Sal had told him it was just a makeshift one for now.

A whistle snapped the men to attention and jugs of water and plates of meat, bread and cheese were being handed down the line to the tired hungry men. Sal climbed out of the trench as it was time for him to start on the foundation. Thalkin stayed and awaited his break.

'Come, Thalkin, you are with me today.'

'Why?'

Sal smiled. 'Because you are my apprentice. Now get us some food and water and meet me further down the line.'

Thalkin hurried over to the wagon that was distributing food out. He was handed a waterskin, a loaf of bread and a quarter block of cheese. He then managed to steal some fish when the wagon handler wasn't looking. Men were sitting back under the hastily set up tents, some lying back exhausted. There was an urgency to the building as if some spell had fallen over the population. He found Sal leaning over a table with some senior masons, going over the plans for the wall. Sal turned and took the waterskin and drank hastily. Thalkin ripped the loaf and placed the cheese over it and handed it to Sal who bit into it hungrily, speaking with his mouth full of food. Thalkin took his turn drinking. The water was cool, if not a little warm, but it was deeply satisfying. He felt it gush down his throat and into his belly, cooling him from the inside. He bit into the bread and cheese and fish, one after the other, and washed it down with another mouthful. He gasped as he came up for air and saw Sal's hand was sticking out. He gave him the waterskin and repeated the bread, cheese routine. Thalkin tried to listen in on the conversation and take notice but it was difficult to concentrate in this heat, which lay heavy on the air, like an extra layer of clothing, suffocating and inescapable. The sweat ran freely down his whole body. He felt it streak down his back and neck. He splashed some water over his neck, knowing this was the only way to stop himself from collapsing from the heat.

'Did you get all that?' Sal was looking at Thalkin now. The other masons had turned away, talking amongst themselves or with their own apprentices. Thalkin noticed Strannin still staring at the plans with his brow furrowed.

Thalkin nodded as convincingly as he could.

'Well, what do you think?' Sal looked genuinely interested.

Thalkin had not taken in a word, not only was the heat impossible, but Thalkin had little interest, which was unusual for a boy who devoured knowledge at every opportunity he had. Thalkin stepped forward to the plans and noticed Strannin's eyes shoot quickly in his direction and then back to the plans. The layout was simple but the scale was large, too large. Thalkin looked up over at the new quarry and frowned.

He looked at Sal one more time unsure of his answer. 'Honestly Sal, I am confused and lost.'

'Why?'

'The rate we are going' Thalkin's finger traced the wall on the plan. 'I'd say we would need to take 50 men from the digging and put them into the quarry, and even with that, I am unsure whether we would be able to do this given the time.' Thalkin looked along the trench. They were on the second section of the eastern wall. The first quarter was laid with foundation and they hoped to finish the first half of the eastern section today. 'We are going to run out of stone soon, this is a logistical problem, Sal.'

Sal nodded approvingly. 'We need to speak to Lord Thomil. A wall such as this needs to be completed in a timely manner, we cannot err on this project.'

One of the men working in the trenches was ordered to travel back to the city on horseback and call Thomil on to discuss the issues about the wall that Thalkin had raised. It was some ride away, so the masons returned to their work. Thalkin was impressed with himself, it seemed he had been listening after all.

'Thalkin,' Sal was watching Thalkin fit some framing for the foundation of the wall. 'Are you listening?'

'I am sorry, I didn't hear it, Sal, my mind was elsewhere.'

Sal told him to correct an error he had made with the framing. 'My question was why do we use rubble after filling it with stone and lime?'

Thalkin focused on fixing the error he had made. 'I am not sure.' He simply shrugged.

His master sighed. 'Your mind has been elsewhere of late, you are not paying as much attention as you should.'

Thalkin nodded. 'I am sorry, Sal. I don't know what it is, but the work just isn't sticking with me. Maybe I am not made out to be a mason.' He looked up guiltily at Sal.

The solemn builder shook his head. 'You have only been my apprentice for six months, there is time for you to improve. Finish this section, I will start on the next.'

Thalkin nodded, afraid to tell him that he did not want to improve. It was just past high sun when a dust cloud appeared from the direction of Scor. Horses were at the head of the cloud as Thalkin finished up his section. Sal had already started on his fourth as the other mason's surpassed him too. He stood and cracked his back when the other mason's stood and made their way to the table of plans, awaiting Lord Thomil's arrival. Down the wall, Thalkin looked in awe as spades and pickaxes rose and fell in a hypnotic flow, men and metal carving their way through the earth as the sun beat down the oppressive heat. Some men had already started mixing the lime and sand to create the mortar that would fix the massive stones and rubble in place. Thalkin doused himself with what was left of his water and fell in beside Sal. Thalkin looked at his own hands and saw blisters forming, that stung and buzzed with pain.

'You'll get used to it.' Sal showed him his hands that were full of calluses, thick and rough.

Thomil rode in on a canter with his son and a few of his counsellors, Commander Billan being one of them. Thomil stopped and didn't wait for someone to take his reins. He marched over to the table. and stared at them with serious eyes. He tried to be as open as possible when he asked, 'So, what is this about a re-shaping of the plan?'

The masons looked nervously at each other before one of them spoke up. 'There needs to be a swapping of the manpower, we are going to hit standstill at some point.'

Strannin chimed in. 'If we keep going at this pace, the quarry will not be able to keep up. It has only just been set up and the flow of stone is not matching our output.'

It was Sal's turn. 'We suggest moving 50 to 75 men from the trenches to the quarry. Our progress will slow but it'll be consistent, instead of the stop-start way of work that we are about to hit.'

Thomil leant over the plans, his face a dark mask of thought. 'When will we run out?' His voice was flat, attempting to hide the disappointment and rage that Thalkin knew all too well. He looked and saw Gregori eyeing him, his hand on a new sword. He looked away when Strannin answered.

'We reckon by tomorrow.'

Thomil slammed his fist down which made everything on the table jump up an inch or two. 'I'm sorry, gentlemen.' Thomil rose up and crossed his arms. He betrayed his real self for a moment but his mask was now back on. He rubbed his chin, which was clean-shaven and smooth, and turned to Gregori, who looked up at him. 'Give me a moment please.' Thomil then turned to his son and three counsellors and they spoke in low voices.

There was activity behind them as the anchor used for lowering the stones in place was being moved along. It was similar to a trebuchet in design, an arm weighed down by a counterweight, with ropes for the men to guide the stone in place. It was rolled with several logs underneath it. A four-man team would run to the back of the anchor, lifting the end log and bringing it to the front. When the anchor was in position, a slanted piece of wood would help guide it to the floor. They had just finished placing the stone in one of Sal's sections and began filling it with mortar and rubble.

Thomil came back and simply announced, 'We shall move the men but we are not slowing down. You shall have the bodies to cover the workers moving over to the quarry. We cannot slow down. Do you all understand me?' He stared hard at the gathered masons, who were considered to be the more senior of men amongst the workers. 'From now on you all report directly to me. Carry on.'

Thalkin suddenly felt that Thomil was deeply worried. He looked calm and authoritative on the surface, yet Thalkin could almost see the concern flow from him. For a brief moment, he could see it emanating as a colour but then it was gone. There was a cracking sound from behind that snapped away his concentration. Men were scrambling about and jumping into the trench where they had just lowered another huge stone. It was Thalkin's section.

'What is going on over there?' Thomil started to storm over, but before Thalkin could move, Sal had moved in his away.

'Lord Thomil, we shall deal with this, please return to your business and let us resolve this without worrying you.'

Thomil looked from Sal to the commotion back and forth. 'Get it done.' He turned away and Thalkin noticed Gregori was staring at him with a slight smile on his face. Gregori knew, unlike Thomil, that Thalkin was Sal's apprentice. Thalkin went to run over to the trench but Gregori gripped Thalkin's arm.

'If I find out you had anything to do with that mess,' he said, nodding at the trench, 'I'll make sure you never work again.' Over fifteen men were now trying to hall the slab up, while others were scooping out the lime mortar before it dried, and with the sun beaming down, they didn't have long. Thalkin threw off Gregori's arm and stared him down. Gregori simply sneered and turned to his horse.

Thalkin ran to the men gathered around the trench and began helping them. The frame-work had not been sized properly or fixed in place. The stone slab had knocked the frame-work aside and the lime mortar had spilled. If they had built the wall around it, there would have been a huge weak point in the wall for any attackers. They managed to haul the stone slab out and began to clear the rubble and mortar that had lodged underneath it. Everyone tried their best, but some of it had already dried. Thalkin was in the trench, hacking at the dried mortar with a pickaxe. It was sunset before they finally cleared out the trench. The stone slab was put back in place after the correct framework had been set up. The team had started to work on lowering the next stone for the foundation of the wall. As Thalkin and Sal moved to start work on their next section Strannin, and a few other masons walked over.

Everyone was red-faced and sweat was dripping freely from them. 'You know how much your apprentice has cost us? Hours, maybe days.' Strannin had an edge to his voice that Thalkin didn't like.

'You are over-estimating the damage Strannin, it is fixed now and we are moving forward once again.' Sal's head was down watching Thalkin work on his framework. He reached out and made a slight improvement to his work. Thalkin's attention kept switching from his work to the group of masons standing over them. 'Concentrate, apprentice.'

'We'll be lucky if he doesn't bring the whole wall down upon us when it is up.'

'Strannin, you are far from an expert. In fact, how many accidents have you caused since arriving in Scor. I can count them on my hand.'

'You insult my craftmanship?' Strannin moved forward, Thalkin saw his shadow move closer.

'No more than you to Thalkin.' Sal's voice was calm, like always, but his apprentice knew a fight was coming.

'He deserves no respect, an orphan building this great wall. It was disrespectful to our trade to allow him to build a pig sty.' Strannin crossed the line.

Sal was up, his huge bulk knocking into Strannin whose balance wavered but quickly recovered. He snarled at Sal.

'You, leave now.'

'Sal, listen,' another mason, who was at the table with Thomil joined in, his voice was much calmer, almost apologetic. 'We respect you, we do. Even Thalkin, he works hard. Yet he is not a mason and he is costing us.'

Sal's eyes never moved from Strannin, while Thalkin was standing in the trench feeling helpless. He felt such shame but something even worse, he knew the men were speaking the truth.

Strannin backed away ever so slightly and his voice sounded almost imperceptibly softer 'We are building something for masons, never before have we had so much work or been left to create our own way of doing things. How many towns have you worked on where a foreman has loomed over and judged your craft?'

Sal was silent.

'Thomil has just said that we report directly to him. We are free, Sal.' He put his hand on Sal's shoulder who visibly stiffened. Thalkin saw his fist clench, he wasn't even listening to Strannin. 'We cannot risk this.' His eyes fell on Thalkin for the first time. 'For anything.'

Sal moved shifting the weight of his feet, ready to throw an uppercut, most likely aimed directly at Strannin's chin. A hand stopped him. Thalkin had reached out and pulled himself up from the trench.

'Sal, they're right.' Thalkin felt a mix of shame but also a strange sense of relief. He was thankful that maybe he wouldn't have to be a mason anymore.

Sal's eyes were wide, his mouth slightly open. His head snapped towards the gathered group of masons. Thalkin was glad that they were out of earshot of any of the other hands and labourers. 'Leave us.'

They nodded their understanding. Strannin walked away, but his head kept turning back, watching, as another mason, the one who spoke, lead him away.

'This is not my life, Sal. It just isn't in me, the way it is in you.'

Sal shuffled his feet and looked up at the lowering sun. 'We are finished for the day. Let us discuss this at home.'

'What happened?' Rosalind saw the faces of the master and apprentice and knew that something was amiss.

A dim glow of blue stretched across the sky as the sun's light vainly tried to keep the world illuminated as the Black Moon pulled it down past the horizon. A few shadowed clouds could be seen out of the kitchen window. Despite the heat of the day, the inside of the house was relatively cool. Sal walked over and dropped his gloves on the table before reaching over to kiss Rosalind on her cheek.

'Thalkin has something to discuss.' He pulled out a chair and sat down, the wooden seat creaking under his bulk. He let out a breath and Thalkin noticed the man's age. Rosalind placed a bowl of stew in front of Sal, another in front of Thalkin's seat, and a plate of bread in the middle. She put a hand on the back of Sal's chair, worry etched on her face.

Thalkin had been standing in the doorway, partly hoping that Sal would tell Rosalind. In truth Thalkin had not actually said the words to Sal, hoping he would come to the conclusion himself. Sal must need to hear the words. Thalkin sat down and tentatively took a few bites from his stew. His belly growled and he realised how hungry he was. The apprentice looked up and saw Sal and Rosalind staring at him, the steam rising up from Sal's stew was not thick enough to obscure their faces, as much as Thalkin wished it could.

'For some time after starting to work with Sal, I have realised that masonry just isn't the life for me. I know I am young but I have done a few things in this town which I have enjoyed but...' Again he hoped that they would nod their heads and understand but it was obvious they both wanted to hear Thalkin actually say it himself. 'I don't want to be an apprentice anymore.'

Sal's face was unreadable. Yet just like before, when he watched the air turn almost a colour around Lord Thomil, Thalkin could sense the sadness that was emanating from Sal. It wasn't a colour but a mixture of sound and sight, another sense that Thalkin felt when he was being followed or watched. It pained Thalkin to know that Sal was hurting.

Rosalind looked between the two. 'You have been working with Sal for nearly a year now, why the sudden change?'

Sal stood up quickly. 'It's that blasted Strannin, greedy and arrogant. He mocked Thalkin for a mistake, one that any apprentice could make. It was harder as the senior masons were there. Thalkin did not deserve to be spoken to that way.'

'So what will you do?' Rosalind asked sadly.

'I can still work the trenches.'

'But what about after that Thalkin? We are about to create something great, a guild of masons. The first of its kind in Duria. As my apprentice, you would not have much to worry about in life.'

'I really appreciate everything you have done for me, truly I do. Yet you saw what happened today. A mistake that anyone could have made, which meant that I was no longer your apprentice, but simply the Orphan of Scor. It's all I'll ever be to these people. You both know, we have been out together and no matter how many smiles and nods of respect you both get, faces turn sour when they look upon me. You have seen this for yourselves, so please do not lie.'

Thalkin began to silently cry, he was so frustrated by his circumstances. Even when he had been gifted the opportunity to live a normal happy life, he could not make it work. If he had just enjoyed masonry, it would be OK. Thalkin didn't mind that he was being treated like dirt because it meant he could skulk and not be seen, learn everyone's secrets and use them against them. That is what he enjoyed. Yet as a normal citizen of Scor, people were forced to look at him; a reminder of the burdens they must carry as the city moved forward. Strange, as he was one of the men who was building it, but the old ways are the hardest to change, it seems.

Rosalind was wiping her tears away too. 'So, what now? You are going to leave us?'

Thalkin shrugged. 'I don't know what the future holds, Rosalind.'

Rosalind looked aghast and her voice rose slightly as she said, 'Well, what are you going to do?'

Thalkin knew it was time. There had been a voice in the back of his mind telling him that this was not his life. Something else was out there. 'I have been offered training.'

Even Sal's brow furrowed. 'Training? In what?' Thalkin couldn't hear any jealousy, but that didn't mean it wasn't there.

'Swordsmanship. I have had a few lessons in the art of the blade and I am good at it. I think this is what I want to do.'

Rosalind's jaw could not have dropped any lower. 'Swapping a good, honest job for training in how to use a sword. What good will that do in the world?'

Thalkin hadn't thought this through to be fair. He just knew he was good at it. Sal was looking at him, his dark eyes shining, as he held back the tears. Thalkin shrugged again. 'The town guard maybe? Yes, the town guard. I can meet all the newcomers. I'll be the face of the city and if there is any trouble, I'll help solve it. People might actually respect me.' He was lying to himself now, but the thought of bashing some drunk's head could be fun.

His two guardians did not look convinced.

'Listen, I am good, really good. I have only had a few lessons but I have been fighting all my life. Ranic owes me a favour too, he could help me.'

'And who is this master that is to train you?' Rosalind asked, her hands on her hips, as she ignored the tears slowly moving down her face.

'Her name is Edelia, you may have seen her around; tall, lithe and armed. Grey hair?'

Rosalind shook her head. 'No. No, Thalkin. She does not look right, she is always watching. I see her one moment, the next she's gone. I do not trust her.'

'What does she want from you?' Thalkin and Rosalind turned to Sal. It must have been his time to speak now.

Thalkin remembered his promise and decided not to tell them. 'I was in a fight with Gregori, she saved me as he was threatening me with a sword. Before she stepped in, she watched me defend myself. She was impressed and wants to make me better,' he shrugged.

'And want's nothing in return?' Sal's eyes bore into Thalkin's

Thalkin shrugged again. 'I didn't ask.'

Sal drummed his fingers on the table. 'This is what you want?

'No Sal, he cannot do this. We do not know this woman, why she is training him, and what Thalkin is going to do with this skill!' Thalkin had never heard Rosalind shout at Sal before. She looked so worried.

'He is our ward, Rosalind, but not for long. Soon he will be his own man and now is the time for him to make these decisions for himself.' Sal reached out to take Rosalind's hand but she backed away.

'So that's it, then?' She looked between Sal and Thalkin, anger and worry smearing her features. Sal just stared at the floor and Thalkin looked sadly back at her. Rosalind threw her hands up in the air and stormed out. He heard her slam the door behind her.

Everything was still and silent except for Sal's fingers drumming on the table. Thalkin wanted to say something. He felt so awkward just sitting at the table with uneaten food in front of him. He nodded to no one and made to leave.

'When will you train, Thalkin? You still have to work in the day, so when will you train?' Sal was staring at the floor, looking like a failed father.

'Dusk,' Thalkin replied. He was expecting Sal to say something else but he merely sat there. Thalkin thought it best to leave him with his thoughts. He made for the door to go to Edelia's to inform her he would take her up on her offer. As he reached for the door handle he heard sobbing coming from Rosalind and Sal's chambers. He did feel guilty, but he no longer wanted to be forced into a life that he did not want. Even though Sal and Rosalind's intentions were good, Thalkin felt they were just like everyone else in Scor in a way. Telling him his position rather than letting him decide it for himself. With that thought, he gripped the handle and turned and marched out into the cooling evening air. A breeze was pushing through the town and Thalkin could smell the beginnings of autumn in the wind.

Chapter Eight

Thalkin retreated as Edelia's attack pressed. An iron blade came arcing from above, and then whipped from the right before striking at his chest. Thalkin's blade rang around the glade as he blocked these attacks, backing away as each strike was made. Thalkin was breathing deeply, sucking in as much air as possible as Edelia circled around him, her head down and eyes peering up. Her sword was down at her side and a smiled crept over her lips. As quick as a flash of lightning, Edelia pushed into him. A low attack arched upwards to Thalkin's chin, but rather than block it, he rolled away. As he rose, Edelia was on him, the pommel of her sword striking Thalkin in the jaw. He reeled back, and felt his whole body falling through the air, followed by a wet thump as he met the ground. His eyes flashed open, the canopy of trees was waving at him as the gentle wind brought autumn. He leapt up, sword with two hands as he held it at his waist so that it covered his body and face. Edelia called this the mid-guard, it was not ideal for striking but the best defensive stance for beginners. The lesson today was:

'Do not get stabbed.'

So far he had passed but Thalkin knew that if Edelia had wanted him dead she would have driven her sword right through his neck as he lay momentarily unconscious. Then again, she probably could have done that many times today. Edelia was standing a few feet away, leaning on her sword, and shaking her head, barely looking out of breath.

'Never take your eyes off the enemy.' There was a clatter in the bushes as a rabbit bolted for cover. Thalkin's eyes had shot to the movement and a sharp pain erupted on the side of his head. 'What did I just say?' Edelia reproached Thalkin after throwing a stone at him.

'I don't consider you an enemy,' Thalkin said, rubbing his sore head and jaw. Edelia did not respond but instead lunged for his stomach, but he was quick and whipped her blade away. The old veteran's balance was superb and she stopped herself following through, before leaning back as Thalkin's blade hissed at the space where her chest was moments ago. She kicked out and caught Thalkin in the stomach. He doubled over but brought his sword high and blocked Edelia's overhead strike, then burst up, going on the offensive. Striking once to the left, once to the right, he tried for a dummy overhead strike and then came back to the left but Edelia blocked every attempt. Thalkin followed with a mid-strike to her right, the same as before, but rolled his wrist so that his sword came low. It passed her guard and the blade struck Edelia on the side with a whack. The two stopped suddenly, both of their mouths were agape. The wrappings on the blades prevented any severe injuries, with bruises being the only mark of their spars, and Thalkin generally was the only one suffering them, except for today.

'Well done, Thalkin!' Edelia exclaimed.

'Thank you,' Thalkin stammered, unsure of what had happened. He shook his head. 'It was only a glance though, it would have barely cut through your leather. I need more strength.'

Edelia nodded, gesturing for Thalkin to lift his weapon. He did and she stepped into his guard, trying to open him up. Thalkin was ready for it and pivoted to the side, slashing at her back. Edelia easily ducked under the wrapped blade and brought her sword up in a sweeping arc. Thalkin knew better and backed away, giving the two some space. 'The human body, is just flesh and meat Thalkin. Our blood is kept inside us by a thin layer of skin.' She was only slightly out of breath. Thalkin marvelled at her agility, vitality and strength, given her age. Her wrinkled face was free of scars but she had a hard stern look about her that gave off years of experience. She crept up step by step to Thalkin, holding the blade with one hand and pointed it straight at Thalkin. 'All you need---' She flicked at his blade and pounced again. Thalkin tried to dodge to the side again but Edelia swivelled on the balls of her feet and closed down his escape. She swung her blade with a back-spin that Thalkin awkwardly blocked and made him stumble. He now only had one hand off the hilt and Edelia swiped hard at his sword. It blew his guard right open and she came face to face with the apprentice, smirking 'Is an inch,' she said, her eyes pointed downwards. Thalkin looked down at the dagger that was prodding his skin. He moved away and a trickle of blood was left on the dagger. 'Your blade only has to sink a few inches in and most people will see their body collapse from the shock. Fighters like you and me,' she shrugged her shoulders indicating that trained fighters fare a lot better.

'Why would you ever fight someone who isn't a trained fighter?' Thalkin pressed down on the small pin-prick of blood that was coming from the side of his ribs where the dagger had pierced, and grimaced at the pain. He again marvelled at how skilled Edelia was. Her ability to use her blade to merely prove a point without injuring Thalkin demonstrated her abilities.

Edelia wiped her blade before sheathing it again. 'Well, in a war you will mainly be fighting against levies. Ageing enlisted men and boys who have only held a spear for fun. Or, in my line of work, you come across a lot of poor farm boys who only have their father's ancient rusting family sword to their name and decide to make it as a sellsword. Most people don't want to fight so they don't practice. As a town guard, that's what you'll be mostly dealing with and they'll drop before your weapon has even drank from their blood.' She smiled wickedly, which Thalkin couldn't help but reciprocate.

'Again?' Thalkin asked, Edelia nodded and they began sparring again. After another hour of back and forth, with lessons being learned and bruises appearing, mainly on Thalkin, Edelia paused.

'How did you know how to do that? You rolled your wrist, changing the direction of your attack. I haven't gone over those manoeuvres yet.'

Thalkin took this moment to take some deep breaths and wipe the sweat from his brow. Autumn was starting and the days were getting shorter, but as cool as it was, he was drenched in sweat. 'I have been on the receiving end of that move a few times, plus I just felt it. Like I had done it before. Does that make sense?'

Edelia nodded knowingly. 'We've seen this before, during our first lesson. You have good instincts Thalkin. Your skills are rapidly growing. We have only been training two tennights and already you are becoming a skilled swordsman.' An owl hooted from nearby. 'Hmm, I think that is a good time to retire. The low light will make it harder for us to see our attacks. Even with the talent you are showing, night fighting is another lesson for another day.'

They unwrapped their weapons and moved over to the boulder on which they kept their belongings. Thalkin had brought a spare shirt and changed into it. Edelia took a deep drink of the wineskin she had brought and took a bite of out a chunk of bread. She handed them to Thalkin who followed suit. They began talking about their lesson, such as when Thalkin had missed an opening or Edelia had seen several and had decided not to go in. She reiterated that after every attack, Thalkin must bring his blade back as quickly as possible to defend against the counterattack.

'Most town guards won't be too skilled in swordsmanship. Clubs and spears and some shield work is all you need,' Edelia shrugged

'Will we ever learn these weapons?'

'Clubs no, spears and shield definitely. If I am honest, being a town guard would be a waste of your talent. I know that if I swapped your sword for an axe, you would soon become adept with it without much teaching. Town guards are there for keeping the peace, when a fight happens, it's just numbers really, not much skill.'

'So why do I need learn?' Thalkin asked, suddenly feeling lost.

Edelia was chewing on some bread as she thought of an answer. 'Two groups of levy spearman crash into each other and there is roaring, shouting and random stabbing. It's very confusing and most people die because of their own mistakes. You put someone in that mob who knows what they're doing and people will start dying at a methodical pace. When you see your two shield-brothers drop dead next to you and your spear has spilled no blood, you immediately assume you are losing. Once that thought enters a person's mind, their death is all they think about.'

'And you are that person who knows what they are doing?' Thalkin asked, eyeing Edelia. He knew so little of her, even after a score of nights of training together. He knew she was a sellsword of some sort, something inside told him that she was without any borders. Female mercenaries were not unusual but in the service of Lords and Kings, it was a rare sight.

She smiled at Thalkin. 'I am. I've been in many fights and being in a border dispute or a disagreement between two villages that escalates is some of the easiest work you can find.' She handed Thalkin the wineskin and bread again. 'Everything slows down, people's rusted, ancient swords, notched spears, and wobbly axes are rising and falling in wanton disregard. Then you walk through the melee calm and focused.' She looked off in the distance trying to recall a faint memory, the look of times past drifted over her. Then it was gone. 'You can make a lot of money and a great reputation.'

'So a sellsword is the life for me then?' Thalkin thought he had pressed enough for today. Looking for more information now would shatter the trust he had been building up.

'That is for you to decide, young one. You must make your own path.'

'You were saying about axes, I've seen some fighters prefer that over the sword. They say sea raiders rarely use the sword and prefer the axe instead.' He left it as a question but Edelia chose not to hear and moved on. The lesson was now over.

'So Thalkin, I think it is fair to say you owe me some further information before your next lesson. Agreed?'

Thalkin just chewed on his bread and took another gulp of wine. It stung his throat as it went down.

Edelia was sitting on the rock with her legs crossed, her sword already sheathed. 'When we started our lessons, you said Thomil was deeply concerned about the building of his wall. I know for a fact there isn't any approaching armies from the North, they're too busy with their little crusade and no bandit gangs are big enough to raid.' Her brow was furrowed as she was deep in thought. 'I have a few ideas but no proof. That is where you are to help me.'

'You want me to find out why he is building his wall?'

'He is building it because he can and because of his desire to be seen as a city. We know this. No, it's something else. His level of concern, you said, was almost visible?'

Thalkin nodded, not telling Edelia that he could actually see his discomfort. 'It was strange, his face was passive but I could see he was deeply troubled by the lack of progress. He has pulled women into the work now.'

Edelia nodded her understanding. 'Yes, a few people protested. Laboring is no place for women, too much heavy lifting.' She smiled and spread out her arms. 'Anyway, you must find out why.'

'That is a large task, Edelia, I must say.' Thalkin thought about how he could acquire this information.

'I'm sure you'll find a way. Edgir has told me some of your exploits, this seems like a task worthy of you. Albeit a challenging one.'

'And we won't have another lesson till then?'

Edelia nodded. She stood up and began collecting her things. 'Well, till next time Thalkin.' She walked over into the treeline first, like every other lesson. Thalkin was left alone. He picked up his cloak and wrapped himself in it. He quickly learned that the best way to stop himself from shivering was to change his clothes and dry himself off as soon as the training was over. He trampled his way through the woods, his mind elsewhere, thinking of the task that lay ahead of him. His first thought would be to wander around Thomil's estate. Maybe he could overhear someone discussing Thomil's plans. What did Thalkin know now?

'Lord Thomil is the new Lord Procterate,' he mused out loud. 'He wants to show the power and growth in the city, so the wall is a reflection of that? The official ceremony is coming up so the other Lords of Boras will visit the city. Does he want them to see the completed wall?' Thalkin shook his head, what he felt from Thomil was worry mingled with fear. Thomil wasn't the man to be concerned about what another man may think of him, even if it is a Lord of Boras. A walled city wasn't the make of a great state of Boras. Vadir was built in the trees. The people spent their whole lives traversing the trees to get to and fro the settlements of that great forest. Huge trees linked by wooden bridges connected all the people of Vadir. It was why Vadir had never been defeated or conquered, as the attackers would have to climb up hundreds of feet to gain access to even the most lowborn of folk.

'Most likely it won't be the Lords of Boras, but then again that is not a certainty. Is a war coming?' Edelia said Novu-Optu were warring a crusade, they must be either across the Forever Sands or the further lands to the North. Thalkin did not know the names of those places, yet. 'So, no war will be coming South and even if it was, Scor has Tyton, Vadir and even the Veil to protect it. If it was a bandit raid the palisade would be enough.' Thalkin ruled out a war and ran out of ideas what it could be. Why did Edelia want to know? He knew she was a fighter without borders so it must be a contract. But who would hire a mercenary to find this information out? Thalkin shook this thought from this mind, it was not what was important.

He concluded that he did not have enough information to even make an assumption. Even without Edelia, this question had been gnawing at him. Thomil was afraid of something and Thalkin was going to find out. His belly rumbled and he felt the tiredness in his legs. Tonight was not the night to skulk around Thomil's farm. He made his way home to Sal's and Rosalind's for a subdued dinner and quiet sleep.

His guardians had accepted his path but were still distant. Rosalind would smile and ask Thalkin about his day and Sal would grunt his hellos and goodbyes. They would ask only superficial questions. Thalkin knew he had disappointed them but felt they should respect his decision. Over the last tennights things had been getting a lot better though. When Thalkin asked Sal about the continued work on the wall, he gave him more than a few grunts as an answer. After seeing Thalkin happy after coming home after the sun had set, Rosalind had stopped looking hurt when she saw him. She asked him questions about what he had learned and feigned an interest. Thalkin had seen mothers do this to their children when he stayed in other houses.

Yet this was not how it was. When Thalkin would be digging the trenches Sal would walk past engrossed in his work and not acknowledge him. Whether this was because of his focus or because Sal had distanced himself from the orphan, Thalkin could not tell. Rosalind had stopped talking about her garden and rarely asked Thalkin for his help. Hopefully, this would change as he missed tending it.

The house was still when he walked in, and he stood in the front entrance listening. It sounded like no one was in. He made his way into the kitchen and saw a stew hanging over the firepit. He spooned some for himself and poured a jug of ale. He carried it into his bedroom and pulled out one of his texts from underneath his bed. 'The History of Duria' creaked open as Thalkin began to fil his mouth with the hot stew. He was trying to read a section of how 'The evil came in the form of a friend and changed the world.' It spoke of betrayal and the falling of an empire. Thalkin tried to see if it was the elves who had been betrayed, but it wasn't clear. Did the Godmen come as friends and then betray them? Thalkin couldn't imagine that the stories of the Godmen and their arrogant slaughter in the name of freeing men. The south saw the Godmen as undiplomatic barbarians who had been gifted great strength. Thalkin always thought this philosophy was strange as it was the Godmen who had freed humans and given them the gift of speech or Uthanarax's Gift. Every day, a new word seemed to pop out, but Thalkin's head would hurt if he read the text for too long, so he would come back to this section another day. He finished his bowl and drained his mug. Rubbing his head, he crawled under the covers.

Thalkin jolted awake, covered in sweat. He had a vague memory of the dream he'd just had. He was sitting in a garden with a stream but nothing more. The sun had started to rise, the sky was bloated with rain clouds, another day beckoned of hard digging, lifting, pulling and pushing. Except Thalkin had nothing to look forward to at sunset.

Chapter Nine

Four nights had passed since Thalkin had been given a new mission by Edelia and he was no nearer a solution. He spent his first night scouring around Thomil's estate but the increased guards presented him with no opportunity to go any further. It was worth noting that the guards protecting Thomil's estate were not just made up of the simple green and silver of the town's guard, they were hired swords. Thalkin could tell this by their polished and expensive gear, not like the simple axes and spears that belonged to the town guard. Although it was interesting, it wouldn't be enough for another lesson so he abandoned the farm. The next day, while labouring on the wall, Thalkin had kept an eye out for Thomil passing through. The work had been handed over to the Mason's Guild, as it was now being called, so they mainly presided over the work. The base of the wall had been completed so they were starting to build up. The extra hands the women had given them meant progress had increased, and a steady supply of materials were coming from the quarry. Although he was focused on his work, he did see Thomil's men head for the quarry daily. He noted that they spent roughly two hours there before heading back toward the estate. The air was definitely cooling down now so it made the work a lot easier. There was bad news on the horizon, as a storm could be seen heading over from Gonadran Maelstrom. The never-ending storm that surrounded the great Venashe mountains, which pierced the sky in their eternal reach for the heavens. A few days ago, it was reported that the Maelstrom was now sending a storm toward the centre of Scor, a black speck in the sky on the distant horizon. It was said that the Godmen brought the storm with them, that they were made of lightning and thunder. Thalkin would scoff at this notion and thought it was impossible that man could be made out of storm clouds even if they were Godmen. The storm was approaching none-the-less and would bring work to a standstill. The clouds were bloated and thick. Their grey bodies lurching towards them ready to spill their contents over the land.

Scor continued diligently with their work regardless but on the fifth day, in the middle of the shift, the sky cracked and the heavens opened. Thick blots of rain splashed down, making it difficult for any serious organised work to continue. They tried their best but when one rock slid and crashed into one of the townsfolk, the Mason's Guild decided to better distribute the work force. They divided everyone up into small teams and gave them tasks throughout the wall. The main construction would stop for a day but the smaller finer jobs would be completed. Thalkin was one of the few who wasn't assigned. Strannin ordered them over to the quarry to see if any work would be available for them there. Thalkin and a few men hopped onto a cart and were steered along the short road to the quarry and the Fortress of Scor. They held a blanket over their heads but they soon became soaked and were given little respite from the unyielding rain. It was only a short time before they were ordered to hop off and were directed towards the foreman of the quarry, who stood under a tent with a few men peering over some maps.

Thalkin hadn't been this close to the Fortress since he had been reading his books and had difficulty keeping his mouth closed. It was a fascinating sight, the quarry was on the far left and on the ground floor. They had dug deep into the mountain. Thalkin was impressed by their progress. They were hauling up stone and had even found some ore. The ramp to the fortress, however, was to their right. It was built from the gradually rising rock and levelled out for an easy passage up. It wound its way around the cliff-face, rising 100 feet before the towers of the fortress that silently guarded the dark entrance to protect its secret depths. It was generally considered forbidden, as it was Elvish, the people of Scor left it out of respect. Thalkin never had the means to travel to it easily to have a look for himself. The slanted walls were carved from the rock and reached up a further 100 feet. About 60 feet up there was a gap in the walls that spread from one end to the other of the Keep. It must have been where the defenders would stand to repel any attacks. It looked like they had room for several elves to march along, side by side, Thalkin guessed. The four dark towers stood like sentinels, two at the entrance of the fortress and two at the far ends of the wall. Thalkin imagined men trying to launch an assault on the walls but the wide base and slanted rise of the walls would make it really difficult. Before you could attack the walls, however, you had to climb the 100-foot ramp. It provided no shelter from the hail of arrows that would be fired against the assaulting troops.

'Get out of the rain, soft lad!' someone had shouted at Thalkin, bringing him out of his daydreams.

The foreman was balding, and what little hair he had was tied in a ponytail. A few wet grey strands were dripping water as he frustratedly told his men to continue digging. Thalkin knew him as Brun.

'Right, you lads are going in the pits. Nothing too difficult, well, maybe with this rain. You are going to lift bags of stone out of the pit, up the ladders and onto those carts over there. If you are tired, don't overwork yourself. The thing that would slow us down the most is if someone got injured or died so don't be stupid. Then again, that isn't an excuse to relax. As you lads know, the wall is starting to be built up, so the masons are going to be shaping these rocks as they need 'em and they need 'em quick. You---' He pointed at Thalkin. 'You strong in the arm?'

Thalkin nodded.

He looked him up and down and didn't seem too convinced. As broad as Thalkin had grown, thanks to the labour of being a mason and Edelia's training, he was still smaller than most and leaner. 'I'm not so sure. You wait here and we'll see what job we can find you. You lot get down the pit.' Thalkin was shot some nasty looks, but being used to them, he ignored them all the same.

'OK, take this note to one of my lads overseeing the work. He's the ugly one with no teeth and half an arm. Can't miss him.' Brun slapped Thalkin over the head to send him on his way. Thalkin had never had a run-in with Brun and started to like the man. He didn't seem to be given Thalkin that bad a time and seemed to look after his men, even the ones loaned to him. There was logic in what he was saying. Thalkin had known men who would rather drive their men to death to get a job done, but in a lot of cases, would lose time because of the sloppy and exhausting work. He was, of course, thinking of Lord Thomil.

Thalkin jogged through the rain, and felt the mud and water squelch inside his shoes. He needed new ones already but a day like this would only make them worse. Thalkin found the man that Brun was talking about, who simply grunted when he read the note. Thalkin stood there for a few moments expecting to be told what to do next, but was just ignored. He looked around and saw one of the men who had come over to the quarry with him ascend a ladder with a few grunts of exertion. He hauled a bag over his shoulder before pushing himself up. Seeing Thalkin he spat at the ground, snarling as he did.

Thalkin realised how it looked, him just standing in the rain, seemingly not doing any work, but couldn't help but yawn in the workers' direction. Thalkin knew he needed to do something so he made his way back over to Brun. The rain was not stopping, and the workers could be seen muttering to each other. It was rotten work. The spell that Thomil had cast on the people of Scor was shattered by the weather. Thalkin thought maybe this was why he wanted it built so quickly. Before the winter, work of this magnitude would grind to a stop as men couldn't bend their fingers from the cold. The wind was much stronger next to these mountains and Thalkin could feel the bite of the cold. Illness was becoming a serious consideration. When Thalkin got back, Brun was looking up at the sky with a thoughtful expression on his face. He turned when he saw Thalkin.

'What's your name?'

'Thalkin.'

'The orphan?' He looked Thalkin up and down. 'You seem different, taller?' He shrugged it away and went to the table. 'Take this to the crows and have it sent to Lord Thomil's estate.' It was a small rolled-up parchment.

Thalkin nodded and made his way over to the crows. There was another canopy closer to the cliff wall, which housed casks of ale and sacks of food for the men to eat, tools and spare parts, as well as ropes and other assorted items, a makeshift warehouse of sorts. Next to all this was a fat young man, sat snoring. There was a bald patch on his crown as his head hung limply, his chin touching his chest. His skin was flaking and Thalkin could almost see the odour coming off him. He was a keeper of the flyers. Messengers with wings. Thalkin looked behind him and could see no one was paying this area much attention. He waved his hand in front of the fat man's face and dared to click his fingers but the snoring continued. He gave another look around to make sure and then rolled the parchment open.

Weather bad, stop work?

Thalkin rolled the parchment back up and kicked the sleeping giant's boot and he snapped awake, with drool dangling from his lip.

'Stop it. I was only resting my eyes.'

'This is to go to Thomil's estate.'

He wobbled his chins up and down and opened one of the cages. He shooed and caressed the bird, kissing its neck as he slipped in the parchment onto the ring attached to the bird's foot. He lifted it into the sky and it flew off.

'How long till it gets back? Brun needs to know.'

'A quarter of an hour, fast my birds are.' He wiped snot from his nose. 'Drink?'

Thalkin shook his head.

'Why did you kick me, orphan?' He bent and sat down rubbing his foot as he drank and belched.

'Because my hands are too cold to punch you. Will Thomil send riders?'

'What for?' The keeper's eyes narrowed, then wide. 'You read the message? Not s'pposed to do that.'

'True and you are not supposed to drink the working man's ale.' Thalkin was quick and snatched the mug out of his hands. 'What's your name?'

'Graneval' he blubbered, hands wringing.

'You don't say anything, neither will I? I feel you would be in more trouble, yes?'

He nodded, his chins looking like cats trying to fight their way out of a bag. Thalkin dropped the mug on the floor and turned away.

For the next half an hour, Thalkin ran to and fro, passing on messages. The word was getting round quickly that Brun was thinking of stopping work. Men were dropping sacks, tools and ladders, and looking around, expecting a horn to blast that would signal the halting of work. Thalkin, however, kept his eyes to the sky, looking north-east expecting to see a crow to fly and land near Graneval's tent. The grey clouds gave a dark tinge to the land, even though it was only midday. The ground was slimey and sucked at Thalkin's shoes every step that he took. There were continuous shouts of annoyance as the workmen were getting frustrated. Accidents were increasing although no one had been hurt, but it would only be a matter of time. Thalkin did not care too much about this, however, and instead wondered what response Thomil would send back. The reply that would fly in on the crow's foot might give him an insight into Thomil's plans, which would hopefully help his quest. As small as it was it was all Thalkin would have to go on.

As he found himself under Brun's tent, waiting for further orders, he thought he heard thunder in the distance. Except this thunder didn't stop but grew louder. Thalkin looked up at the trail towards Scor and saw a handful of riders making their way towards them. Thalkin could make out five in total, only two had weapons and the others were dressed in fine but casual clothing. As they drew near, Thalkin could recognise three of them as being advisors to Thomil, simple lackeys doing jobs that Thomil was too important to do. One of them was dressed like a mercenary and the other was Ranic. Thalkin's brow furrowed, why was he here with them? Thalkin fell in beside Brun, partially hiding himself as they neared.

'What say the Lord Procterate?'

The men on horses didn't look at Brun but instead looked around at the work. They all had small eyes and thin lips, and looked disgusted by the fact they had to be out here.

'My men are exhausted, an accident is bound to happen. It will only slow us down further,' said Brun.

The rider in the front peered down at him. 'You have one hour. Send your men home after that. If the rain stops in the meantime, carry on working.' He spat on the floor, turned in his saddle and rode away.

Ranic came forward as the other four riders turned away.

'Brun. I need someone to mind the horses.'

Brun was turning to the pit to let his workers know of the news. 'What for?'

'It is none of your concern, just send someone after us.' He said no more but turned in the saddle and rode away. He didn't even notice Thalkin, who was standing behind a shelf inside Brun's tent. He was peering after Ranic, wondering what was happening. He saw the front riders turn towards the ramp, they were heading up to the fortress of Scor!

'Thalkin!' Brun's shout made Thalkin jump. 'Make yourself useful, I have no further use for you here, head back to the wall after you deal with their horses.' With that he turned away and marched to the pit.

'I need a horse!' Thalkin shouted back. Brun waved a hand in the direction of Graneval's tent. Thalkin walked over and saw a few ponies staked in the ground, looking grumpy, heads bowed. Thalkin stroked a white mare and, lifted her reins, placing his head next to hers. He could feel her sadness, the black eyes looking into his. He marched over to the sleeping Graneval, kicked him and simply said 'Food.' The fat bird keeper pointed toward the other tent. Thalkin fished out a few apples and carrots. He came back and fed the other ponies before mounting the mare. He clicked and began a steady pace towards the ramp and up into the Fortress of Scor.

Thalkin arrived at the top of the ramp, and the great mouth into the mountain was dark and silent, awaiting to swallow him up. The pony neighed nervously, and he patted the beast's neck. The five riders were standing next to their horses, holding the reins near the entrance and Thalkin trotted over.

'Quick, boy. Before I tie the horses to you,' one of the men snarled at Thalkin as he jumped off his mare and ran over like a good little servant. He played the part well and bowed to each man who handed him their reins. Except for Ranic. The two stood and stared at each other, before Ranic contemptuously handed him the reins.

'I haven't had the chance to thank you.' Ranic looked over Thalkin's shoulder to the mercenary who was turning away to follow Thomil's advisors.

'You will have your chance. Don't forget you still owe me.'

Ranic's scarred face grimaced. 'Well, call it in quick, I can't have one hanging over me now. Billan doesn't let me catch a breath, I'm so busy.'

'Is that so?' Thalkin's interest was piqued, maybe this was what he was looking for. Ranic noticed.

'What? What do you want?'

Thalkin had to think quickly, he had to word his request without bringing any attention to Edelia. 'All this Ranic, the wall, the mine, the fortress. What's going on?'

Ranic barked a laugh. 'Just because you showed me a bunch of Breath peddlers you think I'd give out secrets that I have been entrusted with. Blast, I have only been on this job for a few months. You expect me to risk it all?' he shook his head. 'Move, I don't have time for this.'

'Listen.' Thalkin grabbed him by the arm, and Ranic's eyes flashed. Thalkin pulled his hand away raising it apologetically. 'I wish to become a town guard.'

Ranic looked taken aback. 'You? A town guard?'

'Yes, I am no mason but I can fight. At least, I might actually earn respect in this town as a guard.'

Ranic looked him up and down. 'What does this have anything to do with wanting to know about the plans of Scor?'

Thalkin was jumping from idea to idea now, his mind racing. 'You know me, Ranic. I found Breath being used before anyone, I know the secrets and shadows of this town. If there are any murmurings, whispers of a knife being readied to plunge into Scor's back, I will know before anyone.' Thalkin pointed at the entrance. 'Whatever is going on in there, I can match it to the whispers, if there are any.'

Ranic rubbed his patchy stubble, his sharp face twisting in thought. 'You hear anything you'll come to me?' Thalkin nodded and Ranic bowed his head. 'I can't tell you everything.' He looked at the entrance, where the men were now inside, visible from a dim light flickering in the distance. It made Thalkin shiver, it looked so warm even though the light was dim. 'You know the other Lords of Boras are due a visit? Well, they are not the only ones coming.' Ranic smiled. The smile was holding back a secret and his look dared Thalkin to ask what the secret was.

'Who else is coming?'

Ranic shook his head, still wearing the smile, and started to walk away. 'If you hear anything, Thalkin.'

'Ranic, I need more. Are Novu-Optu coming down?' Thalkin sounded incredulous as he asked, it didn't make any sense to him.

Ranic shook his head once more and turned away. 'Watch those horses, Thalkin.'

Thalkin kicked a stone away in frustration. Scor was the first new state in hundreds of years. Naturally, the other Lord Procterates are visiting, or inspecting more like. Yet there is going to be someone else coming? Thalkin stared out across the scene before him. The rain lashed away at the mine below him. Scor was blanketed in grey as the clouds unloaded on it. It looked like one of the paintings in the Flayed Dragon. He hated it so much and now he was thinking about becoming one of its guards. Either way, it was still good news to present to Edelia. It was definitely worth a few lessons, but Thalkin felt he was missing an opportunity. He was still holding the reins of the horses.

He jumped on his mare and led the horses over to the entrance. The walls of the fortress rose steadily upwards, overbearing like an angry parent glaring at a misbehaving child. As he rode closer, he stared at the walls and was amazed to see there was not a single bump or crack. The overgrowth that had covered most of the walls had since been removed. They were pristine in their smoothness. Rain droplets raced down in straight lines, unobstructed by impossible unevenness. The mouth to the fortress stretched up twenty feet arching at the top. Thalkin reached out, recoiling slightly when his fingers brushed the perfect structure. Leaning into the dark tunnel, he could hear voices bouncing off the walls. He looked up and saw murder holes in the roof of the tunnel, but no sign of any portcullis being there. Thalkin got off his mare and led the horses into the entrance, away from the rain. He rubbed their noses and stared into their eyes, asking them not to move. They were calm and dry so Thalkin slowly walked away, keeping his eyes on them all the time. They didn't move, but snorted as the rain water dripped off them. The tunnel was long, longer than most in castles, from what Thalkin had learned. Normally, they were no longer than 30 paces, but then again most of them weren't built into the mountain. Who knew what the elves were thinking when they built this place, ages past when they were masters of the realm. His heart drummed inside his chest, the blood pumped through his ears and almost drowned out the murmuring of voices. An ominous feeling built step by step as the words from his book appeared in his mind 'Buried darkness to stop it reaching the sky'. He tried to clear his mind, focused on the task and moved on. The tunnel opened up into a dome-shaped cavern and the smell of damp and rust filled his nostrils as his eyes adjusted to the gloom. Thalkin took in the room as soon as his eyes could make out the details. It was roughly the same size as a courtyard with four corridors, one of them behind him. There was a thin balconied path about 20 feet up that ran the course of the entire cavern.

There was no other cover and Thalkin realised this was a killing room. That's why there was no portcullis on the entrance, it was a brutal room for brutal reasons. Before Thalkin could marvel too long he heard voices coming from one of the other tunnels. There was some laughter followed by footsteps. Whatever was happening, it sounded like it was just about to end. He moved in as far as he dared to without being heard or seen, and could see light was bouncing off the walls in the distance, he crouched silently and closed his eyes, he found he could take in sounds easier when his other senses were not working and stretched his hearing out into the darkness. Through the dark tunnels and darker rooms, Thalkin's senses stretched searching for the people who were talking. Finally he found a room with several people inside. It was strange, although he couldn't see them he could picture them in his mind's eye and the vague grumble of voices became clearer and sharper. Words turned into sentences and then Thalkin became a fly on the wall, listening in on the conversation between Thomil's advisors. He was then instantly transported back because what he heard made his eyes shoot open and his jaw nearly hit the floor.

Chapter Ten

The axe slammed into the shield. Rusted, chipped iron splintered the wood as Thalkin felt shockwaves shudder up his arm. It was a good feeling to weather a storm of strikes. There was a resoluteness about it, an invincible feeling as hit after hit ran shockwaves up his arm and through his body. His back bent from the force and his legs wobbled and shifted to account for the weight of the attack. It was unrelenting but Thalkin had tunnel vision. He was only seeing the swinging, the arch of the attack as it rose and fell. His mind fell into motion with his body, and as he read the angle of attack, his body naturally fell into the position of how best to stand against it. His hair was much longer now and so was tied up in a knot, but it was not long enough to be braided like a warrior.

'Switch!' Edelia roared.

Thalkin moved forward with his blade, striking down with his sword. It clanged off the shield, hitting the boss and scraping along the wood. He stabbed out again but it was deflected to the side. He chopped down again and again. Pure exhaustion was now engulfing him. His chest burned and eyes stung from the sweat pouring down him. The wind provided little comfort as the heat of battle was upon him. Thalkin came low with a strike but Edelia was there with her shield. His legs gave out and he stumbled to his knees. His chest heaved, rising and falling like the sky about to release its thunder. His arms felt like they did not belong to him. He was telling them to rise, move his shield up and raise his blade but they ignored him, shaking with the effort of moving. Edelia moved over to him, grinning and placed her axe on his shoulder.

'You're dead.' She was out of breath too but Thalkin could still see the economy of her movements, still fresh and sharp. She moved away about ten paces, never taking her eyes off him. She threw the axe and the blade landed in the earth, a single reach away from Thalkin. She unsheathed her sword and planted it on the ground, resting her shield and sword arm on the handle and waited. Thalkin was sucking in air as quickly as he could. There was a flutter of wings above him and Thalkin saw a group of small blue birds, silhouetted against a grey dull sky, fly their way west where it was still warm. He stretched his fingers every few seconds on the sword to see if he could grip it. When he finally could, he put the stolen sword from Gregori in front of him, concentrating on the fine craftsmanship of the handle. An ornate marking of a peacock on the crossguard was already dull and crusted with soil. He pulled himself up, feeling the strain in his calves and thighs as they protested against him. He swayed on his legs but stuck his chin out in defiance. He thought he saw a flick of Edelia's mouth, a smile? It did not matter. What mattered was lifting his shield up. He ground his teeth together and pulled his left arm up at a tight angle, his shield stopping just below his eye line. He let the sword fall to the ground and picked up the old axe. The handle was stained with sweat along its leather bindings. The blade was rusted and chipped, it looked like it would have been at home in one of the rivers with rocks that have been eroded and chipped away by the water, leaving behind small clumps of moss and crustaceans. It was much lighter than the sword, however, as it was made with less iron, but it still felt top-heavy, like the force was concentrated at one particular end, rather than all along the blade of the sword. He tested it by swinging it downwards on both sides creating an invisible X in front of him. He tightened his grip on the handle, getting used to the weight.

'Such difference compared to the sword.' This was the first day practicing with the axe. Edelia, like most sellswords had a hand axe for general outdoor survival, but in the hands of a trained fighter it doubled up as a deadly weapon. As she was obviously more used to her longsword and dirk, it had lain stored away, forgotten in her pack. Although, seeing the warrior use it, one would not have guessed this. Edelia, who had stood there silently, like one of the pine trees around them, raised her sword and banged it against her shield. Thalkin's eyes shot up, he gave himself one last deep lungful of air, readied his body and charged.

After what felt like hours, Edelia called a halt to their training. Thalkin collapsed onto the floor, his chest rising and falling in rapid succession. His face was slick with sweat and loose strands of hair clung to him, irritating him, but he was too tired to care. He felt something hit him in the side and reached for the waterskin that Edelia had thrown. He sat up with some effort to uncork the skin and began taking large mouthfuls, occasionally spitting into his hand and washing his face and neck. He raised a knee and leant his arm on it, enjoying the rest.

'Your stamina is remarkable, Thalkin.' Edelia was red-faced and out of breath but she was still standing.

'I've been in a lot of fights,' Thalkin said matter of factly. 'Ran away from the guards a lot.' He shrugged and took a sip of water.

Edelia shook her head. 'This is different, carrying these weapons, weathering a beating like I gave you. You continue to surprise me, orphan.'

Thalkin winced at that.

Edelia noticed. 'You don't like being called an orphan?'

Thalkin shook his head. 'I have been called it all my life, a shadow which has followed me. I am trying to get out from under it.'

'Fair. So, what have you learned today?' Edelia crossed her arms and looked at Thalkin.

'Axes can be as dangerous as a sword, preferably when fighting someone with a shield.'

'Why do you say that?'

'The axe can bury itself in the shield, you call pull this away from the attacker, giving you an opening.'

Edelia nodded. 'Very true but you are vulnerable, you leave yourself open as your weapon is lodged in the shield.'

'Which is why you carry a backup weapon. This is when you draw your sword or dagger and go for the killing blow.'

'Good. However, you must always be aware that there is no script to follow in a fight. Anything can happen. You can bury your axe in a shield, pull it down and move in to gut your opponent, but they could be quicker, lash out with a kick , knock you off-balance, now you are without a weapon and someone is advancing on you.' Edelia stood up and offered her hand to Thalkin, who took it. 'Remember when I caught you before?'

Thalkin nodded.

'We are just sacks of meat, bone and blood. The good thing about an axe and a dagger,' she said, patting her own, 'is that with most men you will fight, plunging your blade an inch or two deep into them is all they need to turn their legs to jelly and all that meat, bone and blood come crashing down.' Edelia tapped the axe onto Thalkin's hip, his collar bone, and chest. 'It

114

just depends where you land the blow, where their armour is weakest. These are skills you need to know before going into a fight or learn extremely quickly because learning on the job as a mercenary will get you killed.' She nodded at Thalkin who nodded back.

'Thank you, Edelia.'

She waved his compliment off and walked him to the stone to take a seat. She wrapped herself in some furs and Thalkin began to put on his woollen shirt and cloak as Autumn was now truly upon them. A full moon had passed since Thalkin had heard the news of who exactly was visiting Scor with the Lord Procterates of Boras. Edelia had been so impressed with the news she had given him as many lessons as he could fit into his daily schedule.

'Elves coming outside of the Veil, Thalkin. This has not happened for hundreds of years.'

'Why do you believe they are venturing out to Scor?'

Edelia shook her head. 'There could be many reasons, but it is clear that Thomil has done something no human has managed to do since the Schism. Yet it speaks volumes about their future plans.'

'Could it mean a second war with the North?'

'Quite possibly but what is there to gain? Boras is doing well as a whole, advancing in so many ways. A war would only set them back.' Edelia rubbed her chin, deep in thought and then smiled. 'The good news is, the work for mercenaries will increase.'

'And Scor will definitely need more guardsmen.' It wasn't a question but Thalkin hoped Edelia would agree.

'Of course, news of the elves coming out of the Veil. People from all over Duria will come and see this. Even the dwarves of Yangtze, no doubt.'

They had spoken on the subject for many days now. Going back and forth on what it could mean, where it would take the world. Edelia wanted to remain in Scor until the night when the Lords would assemble in Scor. Thalkin doubted he could extract any more information. It had been pure luck that he had found this out and more guards and sellswords were being hired so movement at night was becoming difficult. Sal and Rosalind were pleased, to be fair, seeing Thalkin come home at a reasonable time consistently and this had improved their recently strained relationship. Sal was spending more and more time working, so had little time for anything else but eating and sleeping. Rosalind did her best to keep her usual cheery countenance but had nevertheless been distant with Thalkin, like her mind was elsewhere. She had not been looking too well, there was a paleness of the skin and darkness around the eyes. It was most surely the worry of seeing her husband spend so much time elsewhere. Yet Thalkin felt the atmosphere in the house was much better now and was even helping to tend the garden again. This, of course, all happened when he wasn't sparring with Edelia. Every other night they met up just north of the town centre and made their way, wrapped in furs and hooded cloaks. Keeping to the shadows to avoid the increasing presence of the town guard, they found their small glade, unfurled their weapons and trained hard for several hours. The week's end was best when there was no work and Thalkin had the whole day to practice his swordsmanship, as well as other useful skills. Edelia taught him some ways of the wood, how to track prey and lay basic traps, but she admitted her lack of expertise in this area, though it was still useful. Shield work, stamina, strength it was on-going and Thalkin took it all in. Edelia commented on her surprise that Thalkin grasped the new techniques so well and adapted to any new fighting styles that she incorporated. He had kept her on her toes more than once when they sparred. Thalkin would continuously overcome a difficult barrage of attacks with a parry and counter that Edelia had rarely, if ever, faced. Thalkin was clearly a natural with the blade, Scor would be extremely lucky to have him as a guardsman.

'Thalkin, when do you believe it would be best to enlist?' Edelia asked Thalkin as she instructed him on how to maintain a blade.

Thalkin scraped the whetstone along the blade and raised his eyebrows. 'I'm not sure. I've never given it a lot of thought. My main focus was to no longer be a mason and being a guardsman in Scor seemed to be the sensible option.'

Edelia nodded. 'Well, the day is fast approaching, Thalkin, that I will be leaving Scor. As soon as the Lords of the South have had their Council, I will be moving onto the next stage of my journey.'

Thalkin kept quiet hoping that she would tell him more, but after a few seconds of silence, he knew she would not be divulging any more information. He shrugged 'I suppose that will mean I'll need to do something soon.'

'Do you know how to enlist and what trial you need to undertake?'

Thalkin stopped sharpening the blade. 'Edelia, I am not sure. I have had not heard much about a trial when joining the town guard. You mainly just break up bar fights and walk around with a spear and shield. When I spoke to Ranic, he didn't allude to any trial or even how to enlist.'

'You should speak to Ranic. He is watchmen of the guards, is he not?'

Thalkin nodded. 'I believe so, although I am unsure of the formalities of his rank, he is second next to Billan.'

Edelia rolled her shoulders and stood to make her leave. 'There is a little more I need of you, Thalkin. You have done me a great service and I wish you well on your endeavour. Although I must say the world is bigger than Scor and may serve you better.'

'I am not sure, maybe in a few years. I struggle enough in Scor and feel like I am just settling in. It only took sixteen years!' Thalkin smirked and the edges of Edelia's mouth twitched. 'Maybe I shall see you in a few years on the road.'

'Maybe, alas I give it another tennight and I believe the other Lords should be here. You have me for that time so if you do not manage to enlist in the town guard for whatever reason, I shall give you some advice on how to pass the next time. If I am honest, however, you are a better swordsman than most in this city or will be after a few more months of hard practice, so I don't doubt you to be a town guard of Scor.'

They took each other's forearms and nodded their salutations. Edelia took her leave as usual as Thalkin finished off the last of his bread. There was not much light left in the day as darkness had spread itself amongst the land. Most people would be in the inns and taverns that now scattered the city, thirsty after a hard day's work building the wall. As he looked up at the soon to be night's sky, Thalkin thought about what all these people would do once the wall had been finished, maybe work in all the shops that had been built. Thalkin had spoken to Sal, however, and people had heard of the craftsmanship and civil project in Scor all over the land. Requests for work had been coming in via runners and crows for the masons. All of which had been delayed until the wall was finished but work for the mason would certainly not stop. Sal was absolutely correct. Thalkin smiled at that thought, happy for his friend. It was easy to understand why the creation of a Guild of Masons was extremely important for Sal.

After the discussion with Edelia, Thalkin felt an urgency about becoming a guardsman. He knew he was good at swordsmanship and enjoyed it a lot more than hitting a chisel and hammer into stone. He needed to know tonight what he needed to do to become one of the town guard. He only had a tennight left with Edelia, it would be a mistake if he delayed any further. He swallowed the rest of the bread and made for the city. Something slapped against his leg and he noticed that he still had Gregori's acquired sword sheathed to his waist. Edelia must have forgotten to take it. Thalkin cursed himself for not removing it, but he had grown so used to its weight. It was important that he kept it sheathed, however, in case anyone noticed it was Gregori's, as they may think it was stolen, since it was a secret that Edelia had won it off him. He paid it no further heed and walked through the forest as a strong wind whipped through the trees causing them to sway. He wrapped his cloak around him, gritting his teeth as the cold air stung his face.

The town's streets were deserted but they were thick with the sounds of laughter. It felt like every other corner had a tavern or an inn. The glow of candles and fiery hearths were precursors to the sounds of goblets being clanged together, shouting and loud jovial conversations. It made Thalkin feel immeasurably alone in such a bustling city. He didn't want to feel this way anymore. Any friend that he once had had moved away or eventually grown distant. They weren't outcasts like him so the draw of the community pulled them away and he was left, always on his own. He paused at one of the taverns and gazed in at the scene. A fat hog was being turned on a spit with two small steaming cauldrons of stew hanging on either side. A tavern girl came and filled two bowls with the thick broth before drawing some meat off the bronzed beast with a cutting knife. She moved in between the patrons man, woman, worker, merchant, blacksmith, and Thalkin could have sworn he saw a man in priestly robes amongst the crowd. All were rubbing shoulders, whilst above their heads a grey carpet of pipe smoke lazily swirled about. Another strong current swept down the street and Thalkin felt moisture on his skin. The sky was almost black now and he was tired to the bone.

He gave one last look into the tavern before moving off and caught a glimpse of someone in the crowd. It made him stop. Thalkin bowed his head and felt a nervousness building inside him, before he headed into the tavern.

The cushioned sound hit him full like a wave upon the rocks when he opened the door. A cacophony of smells and noises made his head spin. The strong ales and smoke swirled around him like the variety of faces that filled the tavern. He slipped past between groups of people. Although he had grown in size and broadness of the shoulders, he was still adept at being unseen. He found himself in front of a table with four people sat around it, drinking heartily. They all wore the garb of the town guard.

'Ranic, I need to speak to you.' At first no one heard him, as they were too busy in their mugs and conversation. Thalkin repeated himself, speaking louder.

The four guardsmen all looked up at the former apprentice mason, and their heads slightly wobbled as they turned. Ranic's brow furrowed as he tried to focus on the newcomer. Finally, he recognised Thalkin and threw up his hands.

'Oh, my Lord Thalkin. To what do we owe the pleasure?' he exclaimed, loud enough for a few people to look in their direction before returning to their drinks.

'I need to speak to you, it's---'

'The great orphan is here for me to do his bidding!' Ranic tried to stand but struggled and toppled back into his chair. His friends laughed and slapped their thighs. Ranic joined in and they began insulting Thalkin as if he wasn't there.

'Does he need you to find him a doorway to sleep in?'

'His family has beaten him, and they are angry that he spilled blood on the floor so he's turning himself in!'

'He lost his mother decades ago and still can't find her!'

The raucous reached deafening levels and Thalkin could feel the heat flush his cheeks and neck. He looked around and saw looks being shot in his direction. The laughter and talking that filled the bar felt like it was all being directed at him. He ignored it as best he could and moved around to Ranic, bending down to whisper in his ear.

'Ranic, please, I need to ask you for help. I am thinking of joining---'

'My help?' Ranic stopped laughing and stared straight at Thalkin. His eyelids were drooping and Thalkin could not tell if Ranic was focusing on him or someone over his shoulder. 'Listen, to me. You done me a good service and I am glad, but I am getting tired of you. Now begone, I am enjoying some time off duty.'

'That's what I want to talk to you about, me being your eyes and ears. If I were---' Thalkin didn't get to finish his sentence. Instead, all he felt was the ground smacking him in the face. He shook his head and realised he was lying on the ground of the tavern. The chatter had died down somewhat, and people were backing up. He looked back and Ranic was standing, hand on the table steadying himself, his fellow guardsmen were all pointing and laughing. Thalkin moved the back of his hand to his mouth and when it came away there was blood.

'Oh, he has a sword! He wants to duel, Ranic!' One of the lackeys pointed over the table knocking a mug and spilling ale all over it.

'Well, I am one to oblige.' Ranic pulled his blade free, pointing it at Thalkin.

Thalkin sat up and tried to crawl away when rough hands grabbed him and hauled him to his feet. 'Where are you going orphan?' The crowd pushed him towards Ranic, who swiped at Thalkin. He easily ducked under it and came up behind Ranic. Thalkin thought for a moment about bashing him in the skull. A distant echoey voice called to him, however, telling him to move. Thalkin felt movement to his left and he jerked away. One of the guardsmen tried to grab Thalkin and strike him from his blindside. Instead, the guard tripped over a chair and sprawled onto the floor. Behind him, amongst the crowd, Thalkin saw a familiar, bedraggled looking priest. His attention was snapped away when he saw Ranic lunging at him again. As drunk as he was, hours of discipline and training still made his attacks sharp and deadly. He sidestepped at the last moment, and kicked Ranic in the behind, sending him into the crowd. A few people laughed but others only spat and snarled their drunken anger towards Thalkin. He felt something smack him in the side of his head, which was followed by a loud roar from the crowd. A slab of greasy warm hog slowly slid down Thalkin's face. With shaking fingers, he pulled the meat away and threw it back into the crowd. It was all too much. The people who threw the meat started to advance on Thalkin. Ranic was standing back up, as well as the guardsmen. Something snapped in Thalkin, so much shame and anger had been building that, before he knew it, he was drawing his blade. The ringing of the metal as it emerged from its leather sheathe calmed Thalkin. The weight of the metal, the leather wrapping and cold iron of the crossguard made him feel in control, and the crowd's look of fear was satisfying.

He planted his feet and raised his chin toward the guardsmen, issuing them a challenge. A moment went by and then iron was drawn from their scabbards; stools scrapped along the stone floor and war cries issued from the mouths of the drunken guardsmen. Thalkin side-stepped and funnelled the rushing attackers in a single line. He swatted away one blade, kicking out at the same time and sending the guard at the front sprawling onto the floor. The second wielded an axe and swung it high, attempting to split Thalkin's skull in two. There was a deep thud as the axe got caught in a wooden beam above him. The guardsmen looked up confused for a moment before his eyes rolled in the back of his head as Thalkin smashed the pommel of the sword into his chin. His body crumbled as his legs and spine gave out from the force of the strike. The third guardsmen was having trouble getting his sword out of the scabbard, so Thalkin calmly walked up to him, his sword pointed low, almost casually in one hand. Finally, the blade was free, and hoisted up so the tip was levelled at Thalkin's neck. He charged but Thalkin easily dodged him and with an awful whipping sound struck his blade side on against the guard's buttocks. His sword clattered on the ground and he dropped to his knees howling in pain. No amount of ale could dull the senses that much. Thalkin smiled and took deep joy in the look on the surrounding faces. People were open-mouthed and silent. He turned, taking it all in. A hot sharp pain streaked across his face, which forced him to roll away from the pain, and stand up-right with his blade before him in a defensive stance. Ranic's sword had tasted blood, a small streak of red appeared on the tip, and Thalkin felt the warm liquid beginning to run down his face.

'Guess this means I can no longer join the town guard?'

Ranic just spat on the floor, his sharp face was twisted and vicious. Thalkin judged that he had sobered up, so squared his shoulders and prepared for a full-on assault. Ranic made the first step forward, then Thalkin, before the two of them ran at each other.

Just as their iron was about to meet there was a loud bang as the doors burst open. Floods of town guard came bustling in and chaos ensued. People became incensed that they were being pushed and pulled, and their entertainment was being stolen from them. The fighting was brutal but drunken. Pewter mugs and plates were smashed everywhere, with bodies rolling around biting and scratching. Knocking into tables and kicking stools across the floor. Thalkin knew this was the moment to escape and so he ducked into the crowd. He ran for the back and dove over the bar. The tavern keeper was too busy making sure his serving girl wasn't hurt to notice. He was holding a club, bashing people away who threatened to come anyway near them. Thalkin shot behind them into the back. He found the door that led into the dark back streets of the city and made his way out. He came into the night and was greeted by winds and thick blobs of rain that splattered into the mud beneath his feet. He closed his eyes for the moment, enjoying what just happened. He could hear his heart-beat even with the commotion behind him and the spatter of rain. It was beating fast like the rise and fall of his chest. Adrenaline was pumping through him and he breathed deeply to calm himself. The stinging of the cut on his face was a sign that it was working. Thalkin smiled, sheathed his sword and pulled up his hood. He made it to the end of the stretch of the back alley and turned left to head home. He was just thinking about how to explain his wound to Sal and Rosalind when what felt like a heavy weight come down upon his shoulder. A hand had gripped him and pushed him against the wall. He struck out, feeling the satisfying crunch of ribs. Unfortunately, whatever pain he had done to his foe, it had doubled on Thalkin, as his fist throbbed immediately. It felt like he had hit solid stone.

'I wouldn't do that again if I were you, Thalkin.' Sal's passive face was looking down at him. As unreadable as he normally was, there was a fierceness in his eyes as he stared at Thalkin.

Thalkin winded himself when he crashed into the table. Pottery scattered on the floor, a pewter bowl smashed and fruit and honey cakes were sent flying along Sal and Rosalind's kitchen. The former mason apprentice sank into a chair holding his stomach. The table's edge caught him square in his midriff and he breathed heavily to get the air back into his lungs. Sal slammed his hand down next to Thalkin so that he was towering over him. His normal calm face was distorted in rage. He had never seen the mason like this before. His eyes darted left to right, looking almost maniacal as he stared at Thalkin.

'Do you have any idea how late it is?' Sal forced his words out through his teeth.

Thalkin didn't need to look out of the window, he had been pushed through the streets of Scor in the dark and rain to his temporary house. 'Way past nightfall.'

'What did we agree upon?' Sal's look was making Thalkin nervous, he didn't know what this new side of Sal was capable of. It was if a spell had been cast upon him.

'That I was to be back before the sun set, every night.'

Sal banged on the table again, this time with his fist, making Thalkin flinch. He would swear that the whole house seemed to move. 'So why did I find you in a brawl, in a tavern after the sun had set!? With a sword about to kill a man?!' Bits of spittle flew into Thalkin's face, making him blink. He raised his hand to wipe it away but a large fist grabbed Thalkin's arm and held it fast. Something began to burn inside Thalkin again. His eyes narrowed slightly and his focus set on Sal's nose. As soon as it had risen it ebbed away.

'Let go of me, Sal.' As if the spell had broken his eyes flickered and some of the deep and explosive rage faded away.

The bulky man stood and moved away, still angry, but the threat of violence had now disappeared. Before either of them could speak, they both turned towards the door of the kitchen as it creaked open and Rosalind slowly made her away inside. Sal moved over quickly, helping his wife into the room. Thalkin didn't know what was worse, Sal's blazing anger a moment before or the disappointed look that Rosalind was giving him. He tried to avert her gaze but Thalkin could not help but notice that her skin was even paler than usual and the dark circles were more prominent below her eyes. She slumped down into the chair opposite Thalkin, holding her stomach.

'Thalkin, what did we say?'

'I understand but listen---'

'No!' She raised her voice only a fraction, but Thalkin flinched again. 'We have tried and given you everything, but you keep on bringing us trouble.' Her eyes flickered to the open wound on Thalkin's face. She put her head in her hand. Sal glared at Thalkin and some of that crazed anger began to return. 'You drew a blade on someone?'

Thalkin dipped his head, it was futile to argue. He knew what he did was wrong, even if it did make him feel stronger than he had ever felt before. He should have left and made his way straight home. 'I did. I knew it was wrong, but I don't care.'

Sal and Rosalind visibly drew back.

'All my life this town has either ignored me or treated me like muck from a pig-pen. Now I have a way to show that I am greater than what they think and still they turn their back on me. You would never understand.' He shook his head and made to stand.

'Where do you think you are going?' Sal's jaw was clenched. Thalkin could see the muscles in his face contort.

'What is wrong with you two? Sal, you have seen how people have treated me, and you've defended me. How is this any different?' Thalkin threw his hands up incredulously.

'Thalkin,' said Sal, and his shoulders slumped. A look passed between husband and wife. If Thalkin wasn't so good at reading cues from the many years of spying and watching how people behaved, he wouldn't have seen the slight shake of the head from Rosalind. 'Clean your wound but after that you have to go.'

Thalkin nodded once. 'I know. I have been here long enough, longer than anywhere. Thank you for all you have done, you treated me like your own and I have felt such kinship with you I almost felt like I had a family. You will never know how grateful I am.'

All the anger had been swept away. Rosalind had started to weep and Sal made a motion to move towards Thalkin but drew back.

Rosalind stood up, and without looking at Thalkin, pushed past the boy and stumbled upstairs. Sal followed her, helping his wife as best he could. Thalkin was left alone, bemused, angry, and shaken. Yet he did not feel sadness, just an echo of something that had been lost long ago. He inspected the cut on his face. Luckily it wasn't deep but a scar might form. He cleaned it as best he could, applied honey and wrapped it with linen. He walked into what used to be his room and gathered up his meagre belongings. He pulled his old sack from underneath his bed and placed his two books, his spare clothing and some honey cakes and cheese from the kitchen. The rain had ceased somewhat, and only a light drizzle drunkenly spun with the motion of the wind. Thalkin had only one place left to go, so he pulled up his hood, grabbed his belongings and crossed the small city for Edelia's hut. As he made his way through the rain, he thought about the bedraggled priest he'd seen in the tavern, with the patchy uneven beard and crooked teeth. He had encountered him before by the fountain. For some unknown reason, when Thalkin remembered this, he thought of Rosalind's garden.

Chapter Eleven

Thalkin switched his balance from his back leg to his front as he stabbed forward. He then ducked and pivoted back, taking one step backwards with his guard raised. He repeated this motion several times before striking from right to left in a slashing motion, tucking in his blade and pushing with his shoulder, then lunged backwards and struck out with his blade. The repetition made it feel as natural as walking. These were the 'Movements' that Edelia had been teaching him, exercises to repeat that helped keep his sword like an extension of his arm. He drilled these movements so they would become second nature, and could be used when the need arose. Thalkin suspected they had a more elegant name than 'The Movements' but that's only what Edelia referred them to as, so Thalkin copied her. He had been watching her closely now that he was living with her, the way she sat down, lifted a mug to her mouth and toyed with her dagger when she was lost in thought. There was a fluid motion in everything she did, nothing stopped in mid-thought. It seemed like she planned every moment of her life and carried it out with specific accuracy.

Thalkin's respect for Edelia grew day by day. When she opened the door to him on that cold, rainy night and saw his tears amongst the rain drops, she did not say a word. She just opened the door wide and closed it after Thalkin had trudged in. Since then there had been a silent communication between the two. Thalkin had risen just before dawn and prepared a frugal breakfast, oiled and prepped Edelia's gear, shined her boots and cleaned the house. Silently, Edelia ate her breakfast and checked Thalkin's work. She remarked on slightly dull areas on her sword, and a cuff on the back of her boot. He went over what needed to be corrected. Edelia left without a word that morning and Thalkin was unsure what to do with himself. He thought about leaving to work on the wall but could not bring himself to leave. Instead, he began exercising, going over what Edgir had taught him, as well as practising with his blade. Several hours passed until Edelia came back. She told him nothing of her day but instead questioned what he did, so Thalkin talked her through his training and Edelia asked him to demonstrate. She complimented him on where he was improving and criticised the aspects that needed improvement. He was favouring his stronger side, and his balance was concentrated on his front foot ever so slightly. She demonstrated this by telling Thalkin to hold after a lunge. She walked to his side, and with a slight push, knocked Thalkin off-balance.

'Now do that to me, with the same strength.' Edelia positioned herself in the same stance that Thalkin had been in a few moments ago. Thalkin came to the side, and with a small amount of strength, tried to push Edelia. With her feet planted firmly with perfect balance, Edelia did not budge. She reinforced how important balance was as she had in previous lessons. 'You will practice this, if I can push you over tomorrow, you will be caned.' Thalkin had never received punishment off Edelia, so thought little of it. Still he was determined to get his balance perfect. The next day, however, despite some improvement Edelia managed to push him over. She sighed and told Thalkin to take off his shirt and raise his arms. Thalkin hesitated so Edelia barked her order again. Thalkin did as he was told and slowly raised his arms. Edelia walked behind him and he heard some rustling before Edelia came back around in front of him with a 3-feet long sturdy looking stick. With two quick strikes, Thalkin's ribs were on fire. He bent over and gasped in pain, holding his sides. A cold sweat had burst over him and his ribs tickled with heat. He turned to Edelia who was putting the stick back. 'If you do not have perfect balance tomorrow you will be caned again.' Thalkin breathed through the pain and, after he felt a trickle of warm liquid through his fingers, he realised he was bleeding slightly. Edelia had disappeared into the kitchen, which was connected by the only other door in the small hut. When she came out, she was holding a bowl filled with water with a pot of honey in her other hand. She dipped a towel into the liquid and instructed Thalkin to lift his arms once more. 'This will hurt, but it will help your wounds heal and, hopefully, we won't have any scars.' She passed Thalkin another cloth to bite down on, and his teeth almost tore through the fabric. Before there was a prickling pain, now it was searing. The liquid that Edelia was applying on Thalkin's exposed wounds, felt like it was spreading from his ribs, to his armpits, to his chest, round his back and down his hips. Just when he felt like he could bear it no longer, Edelia stopped. She applied honey to the wounds and wrapped his ribs with a bandage and declared they would be healed by tomorrow, but a little tender. Thalkin's knees felt weak but he managed to find himself a chair. It was obviously more than just water in the bowl but Edelia did not comment on it. She left for the kitchen and Thalkin leant into the chair and closed his eyes, exhausted. He woke an hour later to the smell of stew. A bowl was sitting before him, with a thick crust of bread. Edelia was eating hers and so Thalkin followed suit.

'You realise, Thalkin. If you do not do these things perfectly, you will die.' She said after they had finished eating. 'You must be perfect, anything less and iron will open up your skin much deeper than that cane. Rest for the rest of the day, read your books. We will have a long day of training tomorrow in the woods.'

It was then that Thalkin realised he was truly Edelia's apprentice now. Before she was just teaching him as a favour, now his life was Edelia's responsibility. Thalkin was content with this thought but his bandages reminded him that life was not going to be easy under Edelia's tutelage.

Life continued in this manner for several weeks. They trained inside or when Edelia did not have any business, in the forest. In the hut, they could not duel so they practised Edelia's 'Movements' and techniques instead, ranging from disarming an opponent to putting them on their back. Edelia never pulled any of her blows, as she said Thalkin needed to know the pain. Pain was important because he needed to know what his opponent was going to feel before they felt it themselves. Thalkin did not feel the cane often, only twice after the first incident. The sharp pain and recovery forced him to learn each lesson quickly. Little praise came his way; in truth, little communication passed between Thalkin and Edelia now, only instructions which Thalkin followed silently. Thalkin's meagre connection to the city of Scor was dwindling. Just when he thought there was a chance of becoming a true citizen of Scor, he had fallen back into the hole he had been previously placed in. It was even worse now that Thalkin's resentment was palpable. He no longer hid the disdain he felt for the town and it was mirrored on the faces of the people who he passed every day. Word had spread of the incident in the tavern and the blame had fallen entirely on Thalkin. He had brandished a sword on the town guard and started a small riot. The only reason he was not in chains was that Thalkin did his best to avoid the guards, but the shame of being bested by an urchin was too much for them to bear, so they ignored the rumours and instead made an official announcement that taverns and inns would only service ale to their guests 2 hours after sundown. Lord Thomil blamed the people's need for ale, mead and wine for the low productivity, ignoring the impact of weather and cold. It was a further reason why people spat at Thalkin's feet and walked into him often. This was, of course, when he wasn't side by side with Edelia, and he rarely ventured outside without her now, so it was enough for Thalkin to bear for now.

What kept Thalkin going was the idea that they would not be in town for long. Thalkin would soon see the rest of the world. Edelia was only remaining until the Summit of the Lord Procterates. The other Lords would soon be upon Scor to give their blessing to the new state and acquire the allegiance of Scor to the States of Boras. Edelia had hoped to gain some further information and then leave for parts unknown to Thalkin. She would not tell the boy what further she needed to hear or why, and it was not Thalkin's place to know. So nothing more was discussed until a crisp cold morning when the leaves had almost deserted all the trees. Thalkin had been outside, chopping firewood in the cold. The air was still and the cold lay heavily all around, frosting the windows and making Thalkin's breath visible. He was still sweating despite the cold, as the exertion of slamming Edelia's axe through the wood had warmed him up. Thalkin looked at his forearm and was amazed at the steam that rose from his skin. He had no idea how this happened but he was fascinated by it none-the-less. He was almost a man but, flights of the imagination still took him and this made him feel powerful. He felt like the steam was his power radiating off him as he sliced another block of wood in half. As he was raising his axe, he heard footsteps and froze for a moment before lowering it and pretending to inspect the wood. He listened carefully as the footsteps drew near. They were light and hurried, then Thalkin relaxed. He could recognize Edelia's footfalls as if they were those of a member of his family, like Sal or Rosalind. He turned to watch his master approach. She nodded once toward the house. Thalkin grabbed a few broken logs of firewood and dashed inside. Edelia was sitting forward with her elbows on her knees, her hands placed together as if in prayer, but she was looking off into the distance, thinking. Her cloak was still over her shoulders as it was too cold to take it off. Thalkin lit a fire without any instructions and stood to listen what his teacher had to say. Her boots were dusty, like the grey broken stone Thalkin had sported on his shoes when he had worked at the quarry and wall. Her cloak, however, did not have the same mark, as if it had not been worn at the same time. Her hands were dirty and grimey, and the same dirt appeared on her thighs, as if she had tried to wipe away the dirt. *Had Edelia been working at the quarry?* Thalkin thought. Inspecting her cloak closely, he could see the bottom was muddy and Thalkin could make out small twigs and grass stains. *Could she have been at Thomil's farm too?* Thalkin tried to gather more information and piece together the puzzle of where she had been whilst Edelia thought in silence.

Finally, Edelia rubbed her hands together and looked at Thalkin. It was not a look of concern or worry but rather a calculating, assessing look. 'How do you think your training goes?'

It was a blunt question and Thalkin was taken aback. Did masters normally ask their apprentices this question? 'I feel like I am adjusting well.' He tried to think of a more in-depth response but struggled due to the sudden request. Edelia did not reply, she kept quiet as she looked at the boy. He stammered as he started to speak again. 'It feels almost natural to use the blade and even the axe. With the lessons you are teaching me, I am becoming fluent in them fairly quickly. I know this because when I was attempting to become a mason, I struggled. It was immeasurably difficult to take on that craft, although I know I did my best. I realise that now, comparing it to my sword work, I was not made to be a craftsman but a fighter.' Thalkin shrugged as he finished speaking

Edelia nodded. 'You are right, you are adept at fighting. I say this not to swell your head but to make you aware of your skills, you understand?' She pointed at Thalkin with a very serious look on her face. Thalkin nodded his understanding. 'I have seen few people pick up the sword and shield and become used to their weight, their balance. I teach you a movement and you naturally carry on to the next phase before I have shown you, as if you have lived another life as a fighter.' She leant back in her chair and tapped her fingers on her knee, lost in thought for a moment. 'Heed my warning Thalkin, I have seen men and women like you, however, who are skilled, intelligent and deadly with a knife, spear and axe, but are slow with people. A great many warriors have not died on the battlefield but with a dagger in their back down a dark, wet alley. They have had their throats slit in their own tent by their comrades. The best fighters rarely die in the heat in battle, instead, it is because they didn't see the truth in people's eyes and hear the lies come out of their mouths.' She looked away from Thalkin and a few minutes went by, both of them not moving or speaking. She cleared her throat. 'It is time, my apprentice.'

His back became straighter and his chest stuck out slightly as the pride swelled his chest at hearing those words.

'We are to leave Scor, at first light tomorrow. I have organised two horses to be brought to this cabin and saddled when the sun sets. We will need provisions, of course, for 2 weeks on the road. Stop.' Thalkin had moved to begin preparing for the journey. 'I shall make the preparations, you have another job. One much more important and deadly, I'm afraid. Once it is completed, however, we will be far gone from Scor and you will have begun the next phase of your apprenticeship. You will spend a tiny fraction of your life with your sword unsheathed. I have got grey in my hair because I have learnt to read people, and I have walked away from jobs that seemed too good to be true.' A darkness passed over Edelia's face as she said this but she shook the thought away and carried on. 'I will continue to teach you how to wield a blade as there is still much to learn, but you will be able to handle yourself if anything were to happen, which I am confident will happen if the rumours of the inn are anything to go by.' She shot a sideways glance at Thalkin with the hint of a smirk. Thalkin dared not return it. 'You will be silent and watch all the discussions I have with everyone and you will take everything in.' She pointed again and Thalkin bowed his head. 'Good, now to the business at hand. You must leave soon and prepare.'

Something stirred in Thalkin, a mix of fear and excitement. 'Edelia.'

'Before I say what it is, you must know that if you do not return to me there will only be one reason why and I will have no choice but to leave you behind. You understand?'

The fear inside him had started to take over all the excitement. He nodded once again.

'What do you believe is the purpose of me being in Scor?'

Thalkin looked away, thinking. He pieced a few puzzles together, and before speaking, made sure he had the best answer. 'I think you have heard rumours about Scor, murmurings about the goings-on with the elves and wanted to know for yourself if they were true. A war may come, but our services will be definitely in demand and someone as experienced as you needs to know how the world is spinning as it may affect your destiny.' Edelia looked at Thalkin not saying anything. Thalkin thought a bit more and smiled. 'Edgir believed you were here to take down Thomil, or at least help him.'

Edelia smiled at this. 'I gave him that impression.'

'For what purpose?'

Edelia opened her hands and looked around at the hut. Thalkin smiled his understanding.

'He is desperate for revenge.'

'That's right, I exploited his weakness. Now don't get me wrong, I have fed him information that will, hopefully, cause a stir in this city, so who knows.' She shrugged.

'He also said silver was promised to me and him.' Thalkin raised an eyebrow.

Edelia looked surprised. 'He did?' She thought for a moment. 'I guess he was trying to manipulate you too. There was no promise of silver, gold or magic remedies for power.' She shook her head. 'Poor Edgir.'

'Poor Edgir.' Thalkin repeated

'So, is that your assessment?' Edelia sat back, turning the conversation back to her original question.

'So far, I have nothing further to go on. You could be on a job for someone, but I believe you would have been more discreet about your presence in town, yet I cannot be certain. These things are unknown to me.'

Edelia pushed out her bottom lip and nodded. 'Good, fair assessment. You are wrong, but you could have only guessed the right answer, and guessing serves no one but lucky dead men. The reason for my being here will never be known to you unless I want to tell you. This will be the case with everything that transpires between master and apprentice. You will know, because I need you to know. This is the way of master and apprentice.'

Now the excitement stared to bubble back inside Thalkin, but the fear never left him. He nodded again, trying not to smile.

It must have been evident to Edelia, as Thalkin could have sworn he saw a flicker on the edges of her mouth as she studied her apprentice. 'Very well, pay close attention, nothing will be as important, and you are the only person who can get this done.' She put a hand out, inviting Thalkin to sit on the chair beside her, and then began to explain in a hushed voice what it was he needed to do.

The sun had started to set in the cloudless sky. Thalkin's eyes closed for a moment and bathed in the sun as it sent rays across the world before they disappeared below the rising wall that surrounded Scor. It was a brief respite from the evening chill. The wall was almost finished now and even Thalkin had to marvel at how the town had come together and quickly thrown up this 30-foot stone construct. It was undoubtedly a rushed job with so many weak points, Thalkin thought, that were detrimental to the defence of the town. He had read in his book on Kalai that the power of defeat can be greater than the relief of victory. Although Scor had time to amend and build on what it had created so even he could not criticise the town wall too much.

The town bustled as people crammed into the inns and taverns, desperate to soak up as much ale as they could before having to head home early. Thalkin had kept his hood up with a warm piece of cloth covering the lower part of his face. This kept his face warm but also concealed his identity, and he hunched over as he walked along, which made him look more like a beggar rather than a spy on a mission. Someone had even thrown coins at his feet, a few copper draubs, which made Thalkin laugh. If he had shown his face and held out his hand to beg he would have been given a backhand rather than charity. Either way, he pocketed the draubs thinking he would need coin on his journey. He waited on the western side of the city, the main road that stretched all the way to the watch-tower that marked the entrance to Scor. It gave him a great vantage point to see the coming of the Lords. Only Tyton would enter through the north, while Vadir, Gorshandrax, Renlac, Far and Kalak would come through the western gate. It was why most of the building work had been concentrated around this area and why it was the also the loudest part. Thalkin thought back, it was only a few moons short of a year since he had helped Momo with his cart and stubborn beast. Now there were so many shop fronts, inns and taverns, butchers and Temples; the centre of Scor had simply become a meeting place for town announcements to be made, and no longer the quaint marketplace where Momo had set up his stall. The centre was where he expected to find himself in the next hour or two, as he judged the way that the sun was setting.

There was some movement in the distance and Thalkin squinted to see a rider was driving their horse at impressive speeds. Cries could be heard from the distance as people scrambled to get out of the way. As it ran past, Thalkin saw a flash of the green and silver trim of the town guard. The rider turned north at the end of the road. Thalkin moved quickly, his head still bowed as he weaved his way through the passing crowd. He could hear people complaining and muttering at the speed of the rider, and guessing at what the message was that he was carrying, but Thalkin knew. He kept shooting a look back, anticipating the procession that was bound to come rolling through this road and up the hill to the centre of Scor.

As he began ascending the hill, he looked back once more as trumpets and drummers could be heard. The Lord Procterates had arrived in Scor. As soon as the first note hit the skies, there was a frenzy. The people of Scor came pouring out into the streets, merging with the few people who were already outside. The people had been anticipating this day but it had been kept a secret as to when the Lords would arrive. The coming together of the most powerful people in all of Duria was not widely spoken about in detail. Thalkin pushed and kicked his way through the crowds, who ignored his rough movements, as they were too enamoured with the mob's celebrations. He managed to get on top of the hill and into the centre of Scor. It had not yet started to fill up but word would soon spread like fire in a dry forest. He had to get a good vantage point so he headed inside the Flayed Dragon Inn. Like all taverns, they were busy at this time, but this was the oldest and best known of the establishments in Scor, reserved for people who had lived in the city for many years, whose families had settled in Scor generations ago, unless they wanted to rent a room.

Thalkin also knew there would not be as many rented rooms because of this, so while people were distracted by what was in their mugs, he made his way up the stairs, unnoticed, to the guest rooms. It wasn't hard to bypass the inn keeper as he was enjoying the revelry as much as his patrons. The Flayed Dragon was unique in that the guards came here after their watch had ended, so it was the only bar that still made coin after the cut-off point. Thalkin, marched down the hall on light feet. There were only two rooms that would meet his needs as they overlooked the square. The rooms would all be locked by the owner, unless someone was renting them out. Then the key would be passed to the guest. The two rooms that overlooked the square were fortunately the most popular, so it was probable that at least one of the rooms would be rented out for the night. Thalkin had hoped that a guest who was renting the room would be less inclined to lock their door as they assumed the security of the possessions would be in the capable hands of the proprietor, and Scor was not known for its thievery. If his assumptions were wrong he would have to come up with a new plan.

He tried the room on the right but the door did not budge when he turned the handle. He cursed, took a breath and tried the room to the left. There was a click and it creaked open. Thalkin peered inside and almost ducked out of the room when he saw there was a body lying on the bed. Thalkin's blood pounded in his ears as his heartbeat spiked. Fortunately, the guest was asleep on the bed, snoring loudly.

The young apprentice, squeezed into the room, not wanting to open the door any wider in case a draft or the creaking of the door woke the man up. He closed it behind him and slid the latch through, just in case someone else came barging in. Placing his right heel down first and gently resting the balls of his feet on the floor, then gliding his trailing left foot around placing the outside of it down first and made his way over to the window silently. Looking out he could see the procession making its way down the Western Road. There were several carriages and an honour guard, while banners could be seen flapping in the wind. Thalkin could see the Red Star of Far, Yellow Flames of Kalak, the White Chervons of Renlac, the Blue and Red blocks of Gorshandrax, with the mixing of the Brown and Black for Vadir bringing up the rear, in the honour guard. They were all there, Tyton, of course would be coming from the North and arrive at a different time. Thalkin knew he had to do this quickly, as he did not want to be seen from the ground below, and he knew that if the man woke up and saw a masked, cloaked man in his room, it would probably send him screaming downstairs.

He pulled out two small pieces of cloth from his knapsack and wrapped them around the palms of his hands. He then readied himself and unlatched the window, letting it swing open. He pulled himself up on the window ledge and quickly turned to his right, looking up. The roof was out of reach by a foot or two, he had estimated. The inn's sign had been there for as long as Thalkin could remember and it had always looked sturdy, but he was about to test how sturdy it actually was.

Thalkin gripped hold of the top edge of the window and reached across with both his arm and leg. His leg found a good footing on the sign, and he pressed down testing the weight. It held. He then stretched as much as he could to get a grip on the sign, to hopefully hoist himself up onto the roof. Someone coughed and he could tell by the ruffling of the bed covers and a feathered mattress that the guest was stirring. Thalkin looked around and saw that the square had started to fill, but everyone's attention was on the Western Road. His dark cloak meant he wouldn't be seen by any passers-by whilst he was motionless, but if someone looked in his general direction he would stand out like a stain on a white dress. Thalkin stretched once more and his fingers tips brushed the iron pole that the sign hung from. There was a clunking of hooves on cobblestones and Thalkin looked to the Northern Road. It was Lord Thomil and his retinue! Gregori was riding beside him. The Lord Procterate of Scor was here to meet his peers. There was no more shuffling of covers, and Thalkin looked down to see that people had started to exit the Inn. He knew it was a case of act now or be caught.

He let go of the window and pushed himself forward with his trailing leg still on the window ledge. He let his other leg curl over the sign and both hands gripped onto it. He kept his trailing leg straight; otherwise, it would have cracked into the sign, alerting all to his presence. As quickly as he could, he powered himself up onto this sign, so that he was in a standing position. Without letting a second pass, he reached up and grabbed the edge of the thatched roof of the Flayed Dragon and pulled himself up. After clambering behind the rise in the roof, he pulled down the cloth that covered his face and breathed hard. His heart was beating fast and beads of nervous sweat had collected on his forehead. His fingertips were clammy and Thalkin unwrapped the cloth on his palms that he used to stop him from losing his grip. Despite the threat, or maybe due to the threat of being caught, Thalkin was smiling. He rested his head on the thatch roof and enjoyed the cold air and rush of adrenaline that was pumping throughout his body. Finally, he turned around finally and found a comfortable position to peak out from and watch the procession take place.

Thomil's retinue had begun quickly building up a pre-made stage, setting it up before the fountain in the middle. It was a humble thing at first but there was a cart containing a chest and other sorts covered by a sheet. The chest was opened, and the sheet removed. Two banners were emblazoned with the golden crest of Scor, a wreath made of wheat that curled around, and sitting behind the two ends of the wreath was a bright golden sun. The banners were fixed upon the two poles that stood either side of the stage. Flowers and ribbons were quickly hanged, nailed or lay around the square. Lamps were lit around the square and extra torches had been placed around to give greater light than usual. Thalkin snorted at how Gregori and his father directed the workers, squirming over how the flowers looked, as if the great Lords of Boras cared about such things. Thalkin did not know for sure, but surely men of such power cared little for things as trivial as that. Although he was impressed at how quickly they got everything ready, it seemed like they had been practising this nonsense for weeks now. Thalkin thought about this smugly, comparing it to his own training over the past few weeks.

The front of the procession had begun slowly to climb the hill to the centre and was momentarily lost from sight as the heads of the crowd blocked them from view. Whilst there was a lull, Thalkin tried to see Ranic. Commander Billan was standing right next to Lord Thomil and Gregori, but his second in command was nowhere to be seen. Thalkin sneered at the thought of Ranic being demoted, chastised and punished for being embarrassed by a mere orphan. He found himself enjoying this exercise, as he judged the people who had been tormenting him from up on high, like a vengeful God.

He was brought out of his daydream when the crowd began to move aside, and the banners of the different states could be seen as they rose over the cresting of the hill. The honour guard fell in line on either side of the walkways that surrounded the town square. It created a half moon of space between the stage and the Western Road. Thalkin studied them as best he could, but could not make out their features, although he could see they were all well equipped with gleaming mail beneath pristine tabards. They all had a shield on their backs and swords at their hips, the setting sun catching the spears as they were held high. He did not see a single axe on any of the men, however. As the honour guard found their position, six carriages began to file in front of the stage. Each had its own respective banner flying high above it. When they stopped, a master of ceremonies trotted before the stage, then bowed regally with his back straight, as if there was an iron rod beneath his clothes. He was dressed extremely well, wearing a warm-looking leather coat with sheep skin around the collar, and a fur cap with several feathers of different colours sticking out of the top. He carefully took off his cap, showing sandy brown hair that was slicked back and tied with a gold ribbon about 3 quarters of the way down, giving him a very formal look. He was equipped with a very long black staff, on top of which was a silver circle that gleamed in the last light of the sun.

'My Lord Thomil,' he bellowed, quietening the cheering crowd. 'May I be the first to thank you for this welcome and congratulations to all the people of Scor for joining the great unity of our states.'

Thomil bowed back, but Thalkin could not see his expression. He cursed himself for not getting a better vantage point, but to be fair, this was the quickest way to the roof, which was extremely important for the next part of his plan.

As the two exchanged some formalities, the servants began to file next to the doors of the carriages placing a box beneath the doors. There was a loud crack when the master of ceremonies slammed his staff down and bellowed, 'First, may I introduce from the state of Gorshandrax, our Lord Procterate Corsius!' From the carriage on the left a man ducked his way out of the open door. He stood tall and his dark eyes swept the area. He raised his arm with a smirk and people cheered. He wore a white cloak with a gold trimmed rope tied around his waist and expensive looking animal fur draped over his shoulders. The olive-skinned Corsius stepped down and Thalkin must have thought that man to be extremely cold, as he wore only sandals on his feet and his black hair was closely cropped to his skull with no facial hair. He strode forward to the stage and stood a foot taller than Thomil. They shook hands and nodded with mutual respect. Corsius stepped to one side as the master of ceremonies began to call the others. Next was Charkir of Renlac, who was old, grey and wizened. A servant offered her additional assistance along with her cane, but he was swatted away with the simple wooden stick. She shook Thomil's hand briefly and took her place next to Corsius who smiled down at his fellow Lord. Lord Braucken of Vadir was next. His eyes darted around the crowd, gazing in admiration at the stone buildings. Vadir was all forest so his city was amongst the trees. Even though he was a lord who travelled the world, it must always have been a strange sight to see such buildings. As it would be to Thalkin if he ever visited Vadir. Braucken was greying with weatherworn light skin but had a wiry strength about him. Thalkin could see the nimbleness in the man as he walked, and his sharp intelligent face only stopped considering his surroundings when he shook Thomil's hand. He seemed like a man of necessity as he wore simple but comfortable riding gear. He whispered in Charkir's ear who smirked and patted his slim arm. Next was Olentius of Far, the island to the west of Gorshandrax, with the Yangtze Empire across the contested seas. Thalkin thought he was seeing double, as it seemed that Corsius had entered the carriage from one side and come out the other. He was tall and powerful and dressed the same as his look alike, the only difference Thalkin could see from this distance was that Olentius' hair was brown. Thalkin could not have been sure when Olentius introduced himself to Thomil and nodded his greetings to the others, Corsius did not acknowledge him. The last of the Lords had already left his carriage when his name was being called. He stomped around the other carriages looking more than annoyed to be there. His skin was a dark brown with a thick black moustache and his hair was cut short around the sides, but left to grow on top giving a bowl-shaped design. Vidaan of Kalak, a squat boulder of a man, was in battle dress and a long silver tipped mace hung at his side. As annoyed as he was, he still showed the same respect that the other Lords had shown Thomil but did not speak to the others. Instead he conferred with his advisor who had walked to the stage with him, as they all had.

The master of ceremonies opened his arms and addressed the crowd. 'People of Scor you should consider yourself the most fortunate of all free citizens of Boras, for before us we have six of the seven Lord Procterates of the Borasian states. Let us all be united to show our gratitude as they watch over our liberty, our freedom and our good health.' He slammed the staff down again and a roar erupted around them. Many people squeezed themselves into the square, even more could be seen in the roads that led to where the Lords now stood. During the cheering, Thalkin took time to scrawl down some final descriptions of the six Lords before him, just as Edelia had asked. He tried his best to sketch a clear picture of each of the people who stood on the stage and claimed dominion over Boras. He used as many words as he knew so that someone could easily recreate the image of them in their mind and did his best to draw their images at this distance, but felt the words would do most of the work.

Lord Thomil now stood forward and raised his hands. The bubble of excitement died down to a murmur amongst the crowd. 'My people, my friends, we have all done so much to get to this point. We have been truly blessed and are deeply honoured to be graced by these great men and women. Lord Lancile is yet to arrive but he will be met and greeted by my fellow Lords. Now, there is much work still to be done. We all share the same vision of not only Scor being great but the rest of Boras. This is why we are all here after all. However, this very moment is not for talk but for celebration!' A cheer rose up from the whole city. 'I have been told that my fellow Lords have brought gifts for our fine city which the master of ceremony will be soon giving out.' Thomil turned to the master of ceremonies who bowed. 'Good. Now I would be a shameful Lord if I did not have a gift for my own people as well, no? This is why, my friends, there is no curfew tonight on any inn or tavern in the whole of Scor. Celebrate and enjoy yourselves!' Thalkin looked on incredulously as the town roared at the announcement. He shook his head, they are celebrating the man who took their ale away from them and are now worshipping him like a God just because he has given it back to them for one day. Thalkin saw the assembly of the Lords of Boras begin to leave the makeshift stage. He didn't need to follow them for he knew exactly where they were going and it was why he had chosen this position to watch the entourage.

He packed up his pencil and parchment and placed them in his sack. He made sure his face was concealed and crawled backwards over the roof, keeping as low as possible. When he made it over to the other side of the roof, he turned and set off at a low run. His priority was keeping his balance so he focused on each individual step. He hoped to beat the Lords to their destination and by taking the rooves rather than the packed streets below, he would accomplish this, but he still had to be quick. When he could afford to sacrifice safety for speed he did. He swung, jumped, crawled and dashed. Hopping, ducking and sliding past chimneys and random obstacles, like bird cages, washing lines and scaffolding, until he slid to a stop. He had been traveling north-east along the walkway below, which wound through the city. He needed to get over to the northern gate and his time with the masons meant he knew which parts of the city were under construction, so he could use the scaffolding to assist him jumping from one side of the street to the other. An old dilapidated building leaned out over the street and was in danger of crashing into the buildings on the other side of the road. However, work had begun to renovate the building into a three-storey warehouse. Hooks were being fitted to help lift produce from the back of the wagons into the building. Thalkin climbed in between the scaffolding and grabbed hold of the rope that had been fixed onto the hook. He began to lower himself several feet and pushed off with his legs against the soon-to-be warehouse. There were only a few passers-by below and they were all so excited to begin the celebrations they did not noticed the caped boy swing into the middle of the road. Using the momentum of the rope carrying him forward, he let go and flew through the air before grabbing onto the thatched roof of the building across from him. He caught the roof with his waist and let out an audible 'Oof' He lifted his legs over and stepped up, then allowed himself a few seconds to rub his aching midriff, as there must have been some slate underneath the thatching. He took a deep breath and set off again, knowing there would be a few more bruisers by the end of the day.

By the time he arrived at the Northern gate, it was late in the day but Thalkin knew he had made good time. The procession for the Lord Procterate of Tyton had not yet arrived. He climbed down to ground level a few blocks earlier and made his way into the street lowering his hood and face covering. Just as he thought, there were only a few people around, yet the festivities could be heard distantly behind him, the cheering sounded so very far away. The guards up ahead would be lax as the more experienced and disciplined men would be towards the Western gate and in the centre of town. Yet they would still be on high alert as an important guest was to be coming soon so Thalkin still had to focus. He walked with purpose as the wall towered overhead. The interior of the wall was dark with shadow as the sun began to droop in the sky. Outside the open portcullis, Thalkin looked for the guards. Three stood idly by, their spears resting in the crooks of the arms as they chatted lethargically.

'Guards!' Thalkin picked up his pace in order to look rushed. They jumped at the sound of his voice, one even dropping his spear. 'I must acquire one of your horses. Master Sal has an errand for me at the keep.'

The guards looked taken aback but the situation began to dawn on them, as did the person who was speaking to them. 'Wait, you're the orphan who attacked the guard!' They looked around to make sure no one could overhear them. Happy that no one was around they advanced on Thalkin menacingly.

Thalkin held up his hands as their spears began to be levelled at him. 'Now, now boys. Things did not go as planned for your lads last time. And something tells me they were more skilled than you three.' He lowered his hands slowly and placed them inside his cloak, as if concealing something. 'Care to win back some honour?' he sneered at them.

The three guards looked at each other, their glances shooting back and forth as they looked increasingly nervous. They were young, only a few years older than Thalkin and they were not originally from Scor. Thalkin was an unknown element to them. Only wicked stories of his deceitful ways and handiness with a blade had reached their ears. They had not grown up despising and pitying Thalkin. Their clothes were ill-fitting, but they were broad shouldered and looked like they could fight. A few tense moments passed and then one by one their spears were lifted. 'What you want the 'orses for?' one said, a deep hair lip and jutting forehead giving him a dim look.

'Master Sal has been informed that tools have been left at the Keep. Our visitors are to inspect it and they don't want any mess lying around. I am to make sure all is in order. If you want, we can wait here until the Lord of Tyton comes, then I'm pretty sure the other Lord's of Boras will meet them and we can explain our situation to Lord Thomil.' Thalkin shrugged, then crossed his arms and sat down on a nearby box, making himself comfortable.

'Awight, awight. Take the black un' he has a maim leg so be careful wif him.' Said Forehead, thumbing in the direction of the hitched horses.

Thalkin nodded his thanks and made his way over. There was a strong chestnut gelding, and a brown and white mare munching on some hay. The black one stood apart and looked agitated. Thalkin made his way around to the front of the horse and began petting it.

'Your leg hurting you? Could I have a look?' He gazed into the dark and deep eyes, until it blinked and turned its head. Thalkin began checking until he found the 'maim' leg. He stared angrily at the guardsmen. It was a stone that had caught under the shoe. It was barely the size of a pebble but it was causing the horse a lot of discomfort. He pulled out his small knife and rested the horse's leg on his knee. As carefully as he could Thalkin freed the stone from the horse, which began stamping its feet and nodding its head in thanks. Thalkin threw the stone at the guards shouting at them to check the horse's feet after every ride. Muttering to himself about the basics of animal care, he climbed onto his ride and set off towards the Keep. The horse was excited and the relief from the pain was evident as it barely needed a touch as it shot off at a frightful gallop. Thalkin's cloak snapped and whipped behind him, he bent low and laughed gleefully. The evening turned into night and Thalkin ignored the cold as the wind whipped at him. A light rain dabbled onto his face but he did not care about the cold and the wet. For most people it was a time to go inside and seek shelter but Thalkin knew it was the world calling to him. Freedom was so close.

Chapter Twelve

Thalkin neared the Keep. It steadily rose before him, the red glow of the dying sun causing shadows to jut from all angles across the rough cliff face. The quarry to his left was dead silent. No one worked today. The place was eerily still. Thalkin reined in his horse and took a rare moment to take everything in. Some tools clanged in the wind somewhere in the quarry, creating a quiet echo that whispered throughout this still scene. The mouth to the Keep, forever open, beckoned Thalkin in. He felt drawn to it. Thalkin ushered his horse forward as he kept a watchful eye on his surroundings.

At the base of the path that led up to the entrance, Thalkin got off the horse and sent it back to its owners. It tried to turn around but Thalkin chased it off. He began making his ascent, all the while keeping his eye on the road to Scor. As he reached halfway, he noticed a dust cloud. Squinting he could see riders in the distance. He couldn't make it out who it was, but he knew they wouldn't want him around. Thalkin dashed up the ramp. Even without defenders shooting arrows or throwing javelins and hot pitch being poured on you it was still a difficult climb. By the time he reached the top, his thighs ached, and he was slightly out of breath. He made a mental note that running uphill must be applied to his training. Six riders could clearly be seen now, wearing military robes. There was nothing splendid about them and he realised it was the guard who was checking if all was OK before the Lords arrived there. As Thalkin was turning, he noticed one of the riders veer off, making their way in the same direction that Thalkin's borrowed horse had gone in. He shrugged as there was little he could do about it now. The darkness stretched out before him as the wind echoed in the tall and tight entrance. Thalkin opened his pack and lifted a small unlit torch. He grabbed his tinderbox and quickly worked on getting a light. In seconds, the torch burst into flames, the light splashing over the smooth walls. Thalkin stuffed his things in his bag, picked up the torch and without hesitation, gritting his teeth, delved into the darkness of the Keep.

Thalkin didn't need his torch for long as the central room he had once stepped foot in was already lit. Braziers flickered around, giving enough light to discuss the future of the south. Several chairs and tables were on the western side of the room and a small platform had been set up in the centre that rose about 12 inches from the ground. Small ramps led up to it and Thalkin wondered about its purpose.

'What is Thomil planning here?' he thought out loud. He noticed some food had been laid out on the tables and picked up some grapes and popped them in his mouth. He stopped mid-bite. He had been so stupid! He dove against the wall as he heard footsteps echo down one of the many corridors leading into the central room. Then put his hood up and covered his face, making himself as small as possible. The idea flashed through his mind to hide in one of the other corridors, but he would be trapped if the person decided to march in there. Instead, he crept low behind the furniture and hoped that the dancing of the shadows from the braziers would throw them off. The footsteps became louder as did the young spy's heartbeat. He lowered himself even further and could feel the cold stones beneath vibrate from the oncoming footsteps.

An extremely tall figure made their way into the room followed by two smaller beings shuffling at the leader's heels. A white silken cloak gracefully covered the tall figure. Sharp, vicious features stuck out of it's face; high cheekbones and a slit for a mouth that gave Thalkin a chill down his spine. Large, widespread eyes made Thalkin feel naked, as if nothing could escape their gaze. Thalkin was in the same room as an elf for the first time in his sixteen summers. With extreme purpose they marched across the room and over the platform straight for the exit. The elf stopped suddenly and his human followers almost bumped into him. It looked as if the elf glided when he turned around to speak to him, so graceful was its movement. When it spoke, it breathed every word. It was like two voices were coming from the elf. Before it said a word, that word would enter Thalkin's mind, like an echo in reverse.

'Make sure that when our guests greet us, no one leaves this room, they must witness first-hand what we have prepared.'

The two humans bowed. They were dressed in fine clothes but Thalkin recognised one of them as a member of Lord Thomil's inner group. The elf spoke again, it was an androgynous voice and Thalkin felt dizzy as the words cut into his brain before hearing them escape the elf's mouth. He put a hand to his head to try and alleviate the strange sensation.

'Go now, as I greet our first guests. Finalise the preparations.' The two humans bowed once more. Although the features were alien to Thalkin, he could see nothing but disgust in the elf's features. He turned gracefully once again and strode down the corridor to the entrance. The two humans looked at each other with tired, wary expressions, Thalkin could clearly see one of the men was Franka! The best smith in town. *Why was he here, taking orders from an elf?* Thalkin thought upon the strangeness of this. They seemed visibly strained as they relaxed their demeanour and trudged back to the corridor from where they had come.

Thalkin was once again alone with the shadows dancing around the room. He didn't have long as the riders that he saw must be close and the elf would be greeting them soon. Thalkin thought as quickly as he could, weighing up all his options. He crossed the room and entered the corridor that the two humans had walked into and peered off into the distance. Braziers lit the way, but it was still hard to make out the two figures that rushed down the corridor. It looked like they had disappeared amongst the gaps in light between the braziers, but it could have easily been the end of the corridor. He took a deep breath, made sure his face was covered, and with quick and quiet feet delved deeper into the Keep.

Thalkin made his way by running his hand along the perfectly flat wall, and after about fifty yards, between the braziers, his hand fell through the air. A flight of stairs no wider than his shoulders curled upwards. He remembered reading about the mysterious depths of this place, 'the buried darkness' and felt a tingle of fear creep through his body. He shook his head clear of these thoughts, he had a mission to complete. Thalkin looked back down the corridor and then made his way up, taking two steps at a time. The wall here wasn't masoned stone but carved from the natural rock itself. No braziers lit his steps, so he was careful not to trip. The stairs curled twice before they led to the next floor. A corridor significantly thinner than the one below him ran one way, back into the chamber with a platform. With a surge of hope, keeping his light low, he dashed along the passageway knowing that his time was running out. The passageway opened into a balcony that overlooked the chamber. It was wide enough for a man to stand sideways and another to run behind. It would be a perfect place for archers to rain arrows upon the attackers with enough room for runners to supply them with arrows, reinforcements and other necessities. The balcony was just over chest height with large arrows slits that looked like they would be used for two archers to shoot out of at intervals. The balcony circled half the room and Thalkin crept around to see if there was another exit. At the far end, the balconies' walkway cut right into the rock wall and a dark passageway continued. Thalkin's sense of direction told him it would lead outside, and overlook the entrance to the mountainous Keep. He went to investigate as it could be a possible way to escape, if needed, but distant voices stopped him in his tracks.

He felt cold all over as the panic overtook him. He didn't let it last long however and changed his mind. This was for both Edelia and him to get out of Scor. He ducked down below the balcony and stamped out his torch when he noticed there were no light braziers on this level. He crouched and shuffled to the corner of the balcony as he judged it would give him the best view of the chamber. The voices grew louder, echoing from the entrance to the chamber. Thalkin shifted himself so he was as comfortable as possible, as he knew he would be there for some time.

Armed guards were the first to enter. Men of Scor lined the room in a protective formation, standing to attention against the wall. Next the Lords of Boras entered, Lord Thomil led the way, smiling as he spoke to Corsius who was nodding at whatever Thomil was saying, with Commander Billan right behind. Braucken and Olentious was next from Vadir and Far respectively, gazing around at the chamber they had just entered. Charkir of Renlac shuffled along with a round, fat, balding man, who must have been the Lord of Tyton, Lorcile. They entered laughing but their laughter died down as they looked around with sharp, intelligent eyes at the room they had entered, and then proceeded to speak in hushed tones to each other. Lastly, Vidaan of Kalak made his way into the room, as stoic as when Thalkin had first seen him. The orphan turned spy guessed Vidaan was normally the last in any room. All the Lords took up seats that were aligned before the raised platform in the centre of the room. Thalkin noticed that Thomil sat on the far seat whilst Corsius sat in the middle. Besides Thomil, each Lord was accompanied by two of their household guard, with the other exception being Charkir who had an additional servant. As they chattered amongst themselves, eating some of the refreshments that were provided, the elf glided in but was careful not to raise any attention. He or she, Thalkin was unsure as to their sex, went into the corner, out of Thalkin's view. Even though it dawned on Thalkin that if he was caught now, he would surely be killed, it didn't stop him from feeling a rush of excitement, as he knew something big was about to happen. After letting the others chat for a few minutes, Lord Thomil finally rose from his seat and took to the centre of the platform.

'My Lords, you have travelled far, and I thank you for resisting the urge to rest. I say again that this could not wait any longer.'

'Scor is seemingly not in the business of waiting. What you have done to this village is mightily impressive Thomil. I would be lying to say it did not factor into our decision to enter you into our ranks. Scor is Thomil.' Lord Corsius raised a silver wine cup and took a sip, the others followed in agreement. Thalkin, unfortunately, could not see their facial expressions but there was no hesitation in any of their gestures.

Thomil bowed, smiling humbly at the compliment. 'Alas, with that in mind, I will make my announcement of what I believe will be the future of Boras. I believe you are all here for several days so discussions and disagreements will take place at length. After here we will all be escorted by my most trusted guard to my estate where we shall all rest and begin further talk tomorrow.' Thalkin noticed now that the men of Scor wore the gear of the mercenaries, rather than the traditional garb of a town guard of Scor. Ranic was also nowhere to be seen, his position now clearly obvious.

'I see, more than anything, potential for growth, my Lords,' Thomil continued. 'It has been two centuries since our ancestors stood fast against the tyranny of the North. We defended the downtrodden and carved a piece of our own land.' He paced up and down the platform as he spoke. Thalkin wondered where this history lesson was leading. 'However, we stopped. We reached what are now the lines of Boras and decided this was enough, we are satisfied with our little pieces of land.'

'The march north was stopped due to Commander Kalai, nothing more Thomil,' Charkir's wise voiced spoke up.

'Aye, it was, on that day. Yet what about the year after, and the year after that. The Godmen flew from Duria, and Godking Balefor has not been seen for fifty years, yet we have not struck back.' The other Lords were silent, a wordless tension was filling the room. Thalkin was hearing the murmurings of war.

'The North continues their barbaric ways, fighting for the joy of each other's lands. Men dying because of a dead philosophy, a philosophy that has forsaken them.'

Olentius shifted uncomfortably in his seat. 'I...I am sorry if I have misunderstood, my Lord, but are you talking of going to war with Novu-Optu?' He looked around at everyone gathered. Thalkin could see his face as he turned to the right and saw a concerned expression, even noticing that his gaze lingered on the corner in which the elf still surely stood.

'I am, Lord Olentius.'

There was open disagreement and murmurings amongst the Lords now, yet not from Vidaan who sat silently, staring at Thomil. With his gruff voice 'Lords, Thomil said the other days would be for discussion, now we must listen.' The short, stocky, boulder of a man made a gesture for Thomil to continue, who bowed again.

'The North is weak, Novu-Optu have sailed beyond the Demon Seas to campaign on a crusade. My reports are saying it is not going well and they will be sailing back by years end a defeated army. Their continued belief in warring amongst themselves, like nomadic clans over bare acres of land, is depleting and exhausting their men, making it harder to till the farms. I have had news that a famine is breaking out also. I believe by next summer we should begin our march North to claim the lands as free men, unshackled from any Gods.'

'I know, we are to discuss this in-depth on the morrow, yet I must raise some issues with this plan, my Lord.' It was Corsius, Olentius' cousin who now spoke. He was the Lord of Gorshandranx, the heart of Boras and the most powerful man in the room, thus the most powerful man in Boras. 'The men of Novu-Optu are seasoned fighters, even the most common peasant, use a spear and shield before he turns a man. Then there are the Second Sons, fanatics who would die to their last man before giving up their beliefs. Every other summer sees an Elderman grow envious of a neighbour so he marches on their land and they have open conflict. Generally, it is a mere skirmish with few lives lost, but they have a whole country trained in the movements of war. "Novu-Optu depleted" is a big statement my Lord, and a famine? No matter which Elderman is fighting whichever other Elderman the farms are always left untouched, and the women and children know how to till a field. They are so gifted you could argue that they can Terra-Shimmer but, alas, they don't, they are just skilled farmers. Only those who possess this magic in Tyton can compete. I am sorry, my Lord, but for us all to unite and march upon the North, we would need more than mere reports.' Corsius sat back in his chair. Thalkin cursed himself for not choosing to sit on the wall opposite the Lords of Boras to see their expressions. He caught Vidaan looking sideways at Corsius, was his face showing disappointment? It hung for a moment before looking back to Lord Thomil. The room was silent.

Thomil, however, looked calm and deep in thought with his chin was on his hand. He nodded once. 'You are right, Lord Corsius. I can tell from the look on your faces that you seem to be regretting your decision to elevate Scor and also me. Yet you said it yourselves, "Scor is Thomil" and I did not change this "village" alone. I had help from our friends from many centuries ago.' Thomil gestured towards the corner that Thalkin could not see, and the collective turned to watch a tall hooded figure in white make their way onto the platform. When it turned to face the Lords, they each reacted in their own way. Straightening up in their chairs, hands over mouths, while some choked on their wine and gasped. The elf stood there, it's thin mouth almost creaking as it stretched a smile. Its voice grated inside Thalkin's head as it spoke.

'Friends, 200 years ago we were on the cusp of annihilation. Total extinction threatened my race, but it was your ancestors that said no. They declared that it was not right. Your Godmen pointed the finger and you did as you were told.' It held up its hands. 'Regrettably, just as my ancestors did thousands of years ago when your people were slaves to my elvish kin. Our races have made mistakes, but now we are learning. My friend, Lord Thomil, has shown me how we can unite and build something great. This chamber, this fortress was once of my people,' it said, gesturing around. Thalkin spied a glance at the Lord's and the armed guards, who looked uncomfortable. Some had their hands on their heads, touching their ears or visibly wincing when the elf spoke. 'We built this as we did most of the ruins in the world before the Godmen took them from us and left them to die. Lord Thomil's promise to give this to our people to assist in the future campaign, and the work he has been carrying out, fortifying and strengthening his city, as well as the fortress, showed my people that he was one man we can trust.' The elf let its words hang in the air, possibly giving the humans some rest from the fatigue of having its voice inside their skull. Thalkin noticed that some of the men had doubled over. Even Thomil was showing discomfort. As unusual as the voice, Thalkin had started to grow accustomed to it and noticed it less and less as the elf spoke. There was barely a whisper in his mind now before the elf opened its mouth. However, it was obvious no one else in the room was getting accustomed to the elf's mind speech.

When Lord Corsius rose, Thalkin noticed that his normal broad, authoritative stance was slightly stooped as if he had just awoken from a long sleep, and he had difficulty finding the right words 'My honoured guest, allow me to welcome you to Boras, although I am sure Lord Thomil has done this. Please allow us to know your name.'

'In your tongue you may call me, Malaphy.' Malaphy's mouth twitched into a smile, its large eyes piercing through Corsius, who bowed his head in thanks and almost fell back in his chair.

'Malaphy, how is it you can assist us in a war that would most likely destroy both nations, no matter who wins?'

Lord Thomil answered this time, with Malaphy taking a step back. 'There is a reason it took so long for the elves to be subdued to the Veil. For nearly a millennia of warfare the elves withstood the Godmen's onslaught and many lives were lost. There were many reasons for this but allow us to show you one.' Thomil took a step back so that he was next to Malaphy. A tremendous noise came barrelling through the corridor that Thalkin found the stairs in. It started as a rumbling then a crashing, which grew louder as the sound came closer. Thalkin forced himself not to lean over the arrow slits to get a better view as a shiny, bulky object came clattering through the corridor and up onto the platform. What seemed like a steel horse with a man dressed in steel sitting atop it, reared up on the platform and came crashing down. The horse pawed at the ground as the rider held a long spear as he tried his best to keep the beast calm.

At first glance Thalkin believed it to be magic, a shimmer to make the steel come to life in the shape of a horse. However, it was clear that the steel had been crafted to cover the horse in armour. No less impressive was the rider, who had plates of steel protection, covering his whole body. Thalkin had only been in Scor so he had only heard tales of the outside and had never heard anything like this. He had this in commonality with everyone in the room, including the guards, the Lords and the men of Scor. Most men who took the field of battle wore chainmail and a leather surcoat as protection, with a steel cap for the most experienced troops. It would be safe to assume that no one in Duria had ever seen anything like this, bar the Elves, of course. It was impressively polished and flame light danced off the steel, creating a shimmer that was said to be a tell-tale sign of magic usage. This must be what it looks like, thought Thalkin, and he felt less shame about originally thinking it was a shimmer.

'Behold, my Lords! You wanted an advantage, you wanted a reason. I present you a Knight!' Lord Thomil's voiced boomed out with almost fanatical excitement at his creation. 'Our friend Malaphy, is a master at forging steel this way. In their tongue they call it knighting, as they weave the iron the tin together to make more precise ingots of steel, allowing for full steel protection.' Lord Thomil smiled to himself, almost bending over. He looked hysterically happy. The reaction from the Lord's must have been exactly what he was waiting for. 'The greatest gift that Malaphy and his people has given us is teaching my most talented smith exactly how to craft such a weapon. And do not mistake this for mere armour, this is a weapon.' Thomil must have been referring to Franka, who Thalkin had seen before in the hall. A flash of memory from many moons ago came sweeping back to Thalkin, when he saw Ranic drop sheets of metal outside Franka's smithy. They were steel plates! It must have been in preparation for this. Thalkin's head was spinning. He found himself breathing hard and he began to control his breathing and emotions.

After the initial outcry there was silence in the room. Thalkin looked at the Lords. Corsius had both hands grasping at the arms of his chair, his knuckles white. Charkir had her hand over her heart and Larcile had an arm around her. Braucken was leaning forward with one hand on his knee, the other over his mouth. Olentius of Far was sitting exactly like his cousin. Thalkin's eyes fell on the Lord from Kalak but he was rising in his chair and he began clapping.

The other Lord's remained in their positions, but their heads shot to Vidaan. Another person began clapping, it was Olentius who was joining in and the rest followed suit. Thomil bowed, while Malaphy's eyes scanned the faces of the people in the room, looking like he was barely paying attention to anything that was happening.

'My Lords, this is the key. The key to finish what our ancestors started! Lord Thomil, if there is anything Kalak can do to help. Let it be known as long as you help us crush our enemies in Moosh, you have our banners.' Vidaan struck his chest with a closed fist and his guards followed suit.

'Aye, Far's fleet will be yours.' Olentius bowed as did his guards.

'Wait, wait. We cannot make such a rash decision! Please, my Lords, we need to talk before we declare war. And is this the place to discuss such matters? We do not know who here is to be trusted.' Corsius motioned with his hands as she spoke for all to stay seated.

'These are select men of Lord Thomil, cousin. If Lord Thomil can trust them so shall we. The only thing to discuss surely is strategy?' Olentius shrugged.

'Olentius, surely you are not certain on the decision to throw your people's lives into a war?' Corsuis' faced his cousin defiantly, his chin raised.

'My people's lives are not of your concern, cousin.' There was a hint of contempt in Olentius voice as the two stood facing each other. Thalkin made a mental note of this exchange.

'My Lords please,' Charkir stood with difficulty as Lorcile helped her. 'Lord Corsius is correct, this is not the place to commit ourselves, regardless of your views.' She held up a hand as Vidaan opened his mouth to interject. Vidaan stepped back, his passive face not betraying his emotions. 'Lord Thomil, we all thank you for this demonstration, it certainly is impressive and to our new friend, Malaphy.' There was an emphasis from Lord Charkir when she said the word friend, but Thalkin held back his judgement on exactly what that meant. 'Malaphy, it is an honour to receive you beyond the Veil, I speak on behalf of all of the Lords of Boras when we say that we hope you are with us when we discuss the oncoming plans for our nations.' Charkir made a motion of bowing, but with her advancing years, it was barely a nod of the head.

Thalkin ducked behind the balcony and started to make his way towards the passageway outside. The meeting seemed to be ending and he had more than enough information for Edelia. He had another jolt of excitement at the thought of his continued training under Edelia, the world of Duria was his to explore. He switched his focus so he could concentrate on silently making his escape. Voices continued to echo in the chamber as the Lords exchanged pleasantries, and Thalkin needed to be quick to avoid being noticed. When he was a few yards into the passageway, Thalkin stood up and jogged outside.

The light rain had turned into a heavy shower but Thalkin was protected for the moment by the cliffs overhang that served as further protection for defenders in the event of an attack. According to Malaphy, the elves crafted this Keep and Thalkin noticed that the battlements came just below waist height. Thalkin thought of a seven-foot-tall elf on this wall. The battlement seemed way too small, but there must have been some tactic to their design. As he peered over, he noticed two guards standing by the entrance, they were huddled against the wall trying to shield themselves against the rain. It quickly dawned on Thalkin that getting down could prove difficult. The drop was roughly 60 feet as the wall slanted downwards, to make it difficult for an attacker to climb up, although this made dropping down from it slightly easier. However, the length of the wall was in full sight of the guards at the entrance, such was its design. The rain and dying of the light provided some cover but Thalkin needed to be sure because of the risk of being seen. He gazed back into the tunnel that led into the fortress. A patrol could wander by at any time and even if he could avoid detection, waiting out the council of Lords wasn't a real option. Edelia was leaving tonight and if Thalkin did not get to her in time, she may leave without him.

He had to risk it and moved forward. He started toward the end of the wall, passing through one of the towers that stood sentinel to the entrance. He planned on gripping the edge of the battlements, so that he was hanging off and simply slide down. The rain hopefully would soften up the surface and he would have to make sure his cloak would be wrapped about him to help stave off any injury. Thalkin gave another look over to check on the guards. At this moment, a gust of wind blew at the fortress. The guard's hoods flew back from their heads revealing the men beneath. Thalkin smirked, at the look of discomfort on the faces of Ranic and Gregori. This is how far Ranic had fallen, to simple guard duty in the rain, and Gregori must be here on his father's orders. It was hard to remove the smirk from Thalkin's face as he watched their mouths curse the weather and they pulled their hoods up over their already drenched heads.

It only strengthened Thalkin's need not to be seen. For him to be discovered by his two worst enemies would be the most nightmarish outcome for Thalkin. The battlements ended as the mountain wall curved outwards. He looked towards Scor and imagined the revelry would have moved its way into the inns and taverns. Edelia would be waiting outside Scor. He thought for a moment about sneaking back in to see Sal and Rosalind. With sadness he shook the thought from his mind. They were part of his old life and they had made their decision. He wrapped his cloak about him and with careful movements he climbed over. Thalkin didn't have time to feel fear so he gave himself no chance to think about how high up he was. He covered his hands with his wrappings for better grip and began to hang off the edge. He slid down. The sheer flat surface coupled with the rain made most of the slide down nothing but fun Thalkin thought. He was picking up speed and the rain lashed at his face, but about three quarters of the way down, his foot caught on an outcrop and turned his body outwards. He fell and landed on his back. The wind blew out from his lungs and for a moment he was dazed. He quickly turned over and lay flat on the ground, trying to stay out of sight, catching his breath. Luckily, Thalkin landed just as the ground began to slope down, creating the ramp leading up to the entrance of the fortress, giving some cover. He could not tell if Ranic and Gregori spotted him, but he knew they could not see him now. He crawled down the ramp for as long as he could. It then turned outwards so he had to rise into a crouch to try and get down as quickly as possible. He winced as pain shot up his ankle and then lanced through his back, but he tried to ignore it for now. Thalkin made himself part of the wall as he half-crouched, half-ran down the ramp. As he kept looking back, he saw the two guards casting looks towards him, and whenever they did, he would freeze. He managed to get to the bottom, however, without Ranic or Gregori noticing him. The ground opened up now, but due to the ongoing work in the quarry, there were scattered obstacles which Thalkin could hide behind to block anyone's view. Ignoring the pain in his ankle, Thalkin dashed between scaffolding, tents, and storerooms. He was several hundred yards away from the Keep and could barely make out Ranic and Gregori at the entrance, so he felt it was safe now to make it for Scor. He left the quarry with a limping run. He gave one last look at the Keep. Thalkin thought it could be the last time he gazed upon it. He was expecting the same rush of feelings he felt like the countless times before. When he looked at it now, as he shuffled away, there no sense of foreboding, no dread or mysterious sense calling him in. The dark mountain remained motionless and unnoticeable, like a shadow in the rain. Maybe his instincts about the buried darkness was indeed misguided.

The wind and rain whipped at Thalkin and his ankle and back ached with each step. He started to feel deep fatigue in his thighs and calves. Although Thalkin hadn't run much today, he had been climbing, and crouching in stressful positions and rode, so it was beginning to take its toll. With all the strength he could muster, he focused his mind on riding off into the North with Edelia, telling her excitedly about all that he had learnt. As he neared the city walls, Thalkin turned off the road into Scor from the quarry and into a copse of trees, which provided him with some cover from any patrols as well as the rain. The trees bent around the corner of the city giving him a sight of the northern entrance to Scor. It would be where Edelia was waiting with a pair of horses. Thalkin trudged his way through the undergrowth and leant wearily on a tree. He gazed up at the city walls through the branches and saw no patrols. The city would be lax due to the celebrations and the rain would deter most of the guards, but even if they were seen, there would be no reason to stop Thalkin and Edelia from riding away.

He bent down in between deep breaths and pulled off his boot. He felt some swelling on his ankle and it hurt to touch, but he could move his toes easily so he assumed it was just a sprain. He tested his back and gathered there was nothing broken, just bad bruising; after all, he had not fallen from too high. As he was placing his boot back on, he heard a twig snap. Thalkin whipped around but found himself sprawled on the floor as Ranic tackled him. Thalkin felt his back surge with pain but threw his head and fists into his attacker. Thalkin didn't have time to think, so instead he used all his anger and hatred to fuel his attack. Ranic tried to pull away to get distance from Thalkin so he could throw some effective blows at him. The young spy moved into the space and sunk his teeth into Ranic's face. Even during the heat of the fight, Thalkin could taste Ranic's flaky flesh and blood. Ranic screamed as the skin was broken. Thalkin used this moment to push from under Ranic and find his feet. As he turned to face the guard of Scor, however, there was another blur of motion as Gregori charged at Thalkin.

Instincts kicked in and Thalkin ducked between a flash of punches and twisted his hips, delivering a punishing punch to the kidneys. Thalkin followed through and kicked out at the rising Ranic, whose hands went from holding his bleeding face to his groin. He grabbed the unguarded shaved head of Ranic and slammed it as hard as he could on the side of a tree. The guard slumped to the ground, unconscious. Thalkin hobbled as he turned to face Gregori and heard the unsheathing of a blade. Thalkin threw up his hands exasperated.

'Gregori, stand aside. I bested one of the best swordsmen of Scor. I will unarm you like Edelia and have you crying back to your father.'

Gregori's face twisted with rage. 'Oh, and you know exactly where my father is don't you.' he said through gritted teeth.

'You saw me then.' There was no use in lying. 'Why didn't you run to your Lord Papa and tell him then? Had to gather up your lackeys first?' Thalkin raised his hands slightly as if showing Gregori he was unarmed but bringing them closer to the weapons that hung from his hips.

'I don't need my father or his guards, I can take you for myself.' Gregori lunged at Thalkin, aiming to shove his blade through his stomach. Thalkin was ready and took a leap back drawing his own sword.

'Let's see if your father's money made you an able fighter.' Thalkin's goading was working as Gregori advanced again, swinging wildly at him. The apprentice was able to dodge and deflect most of the attacks with ease. Gregori continued to grow frustrated and aimed an over-arching slash, Thalkin met the blade as it was coming down and deflected it towards the ground. Thalkin and Gregori were face-to-face now and he threw his head straight into the Lord Procterate son's nose. There was an audible crack as blood gushed freely. Gregori stumbled and Thalkin followed up swiping at the sword. Gregori was disarmed as his sword flew across the air and slammed into a tree. Thalkin was not finished, however, as he advanced on his rival. He brought the pommel of his sword crashing into the side of Gregori's face, followed by another audible crack. Thalkin stood over his most hated enemy and hovered his blade over the boy's neck, debating whether to plunge it down. A hot flash of pain erupted across his back and he stumbled forward, screaming in pain. He felt hot liquid trickle down his back. He turned to see Ranic swaying from side to side, sword in hand with his blood dripping from the blade.

'That makes two scars, I've given you.' Ranic said slurring his speech. Having his head slammed against the tree had left him groggy but he still sneered when his eyes ran over Thalkin's facial scar.

The orphan of Scor felt his barely contained rage bubble over. 'I am going to kill you, Ranic.' Thalkin advanced gripping his sword in his hand tightly. With a war cry Thalkin attacked Ranic. Iron met iron and sparks flashed. The two went back and forth with attacks, parries and ripostes. Their blades rang out as they met each other again and again, the two barely giving an inch. As groggy as Ranic was moving, Thalkin was carrying multiple injuries so there was no clear advantage between the two. When skill failed, instinct took over and soon they were both breathing heavily and covered in sweat.

'Having trouble ending the fight, Thalkin?' Ranic said breathing hard, with eyes barely focusing on his target.

'I would be offended if I wasn't fighting an experienced town guard with the flakiest skin in all of Duria,' Thalkin sneered but was deeply concerned how quickly he was losing blood. The gash on his back stung from the sweat dripping into it, and his breaches and boots were soaked with his own blood. He swayed slightly but fell into stabbing at Ranic's chest.

Ranic was not prepared for the move and barely deflected it. Thalkin kicked out and his shin slammed into Ranic's thigh. The knees of the town guard buckled and Thalkin slashed down, cutting deep into Ranic's sword arm. There was a scream as he dropped his sword. Blood flowed from his forearm and Thalkin grinned at his fallen foe. He raised his blade to sink it deep in between Ranic's shoulder and neck to claim his first kill. All reason and thought had abandoned Thalkin. The only thing that was clear was the feeling of joy from ending the life of Ranic. He thought for a moment that he heard a woman scream for him to stop, but didn't have a moment to think as he was suddenly flying backwards as the wind was taken from his lungs. Gregori had awoken and tackled Thalkin. They both crashed into something soft and rolled away before jumping to his feet. He refused to panic when he realised his sword hand was empty. He quickly scanned the floor around him, hoping to see his iron.

He saw Gregori kneeling on the floor. He was not looking at Thalkin, but had a look of fear as he was staring at a crumpled figure on the floor. Thalkin's blood went cold and a rising urge to be sick overcame him. He found his sword, it was buried in the stomach of Rosalind.

Thalkin blinked at the scene, as surely it did not make any sense. He dropped to his knees, either through fatigue or from the shock of what he saw. Rosalind was on her side with her back to Thalkin, a bloody blade sticking through her spine. He crawled over to her slowly. Gregori was sitting on his backside, staring in shock, his blonde hair stuck to his face, clammy with sweat. Thalkin rested a hand gently on her shoulder, as her head turned to face him. Her face was pale, her eyes wide with shock and blood trickled from her mouth. Thalkin's eyes began to burn with tears as Rosalind tried to speak. He shushed her and pulled her wet hair from her face and over her ears.

'Thalkin...' Barely a whisper escaped Rosalind's mouth.

'Do not speak, Rosalind.' Thalkin did not know what to do, he did not understand.

'Listen...we shouldn't have turned you away. I came to find you, some guards had told me you had left the city. Me and Sal were just afraid. We were having such fun and we wanted you with us. All three of us.' She began to cry. Thalkin saw the swollen stomach of Rosalind, with blood streaming from the wound. All he thought of doing was to try and staunch the blood.

'Thalkin...' Rosalind raised a hand to Thalkin. Tears were streaming down his face, mixing with the rain that was making its way through the canopy. Just as her fingertips brushed Thalkin's cheek, her hand dropped and fell to ground. Her chest rose and fell but did not move soon after. Her eyes were staring past Thalkin, lifeless.

Thalkin looked at the sword's crossguard, the ornate peacock crusted with blood and soil, and he remembered who it had originally belonged to. Sitting no more than a few feet away was its owner, Gregori. The Lord's son was still staring in shock, whimpering with fear.

'You did this,' Thalkin growled. He rose, leaving Rosalind's body. Gregori's eyes snapped to attention. He tried to speak and raise his arms in defence but Thalkin was already on top of him. The world faded away and all that was left was fury and rage. Fists were pulled back and shot forward, slamming into bone and flesh and teeth. Steady, measured strikes filled with raw

159

strength pounded into Gregori's face. The shouts of pain and protests soon died away so all that could be heard was the pattering of rain and the dull thud of knuckles on bone.

When his vision cleared, Thalkin was breathing heavy. He felt a metallic taste in his mouth followed by all the bumps and bruises he had picked up. His hands were dull with pain and he looked down at them. They were bloody and swollen, and he found it difficult to close them. He could see a tooth or two buried in between his knuckles. He looked past his hands and saw a bloody mess. Gregori's face was unrecognisable. His mouth opened and closed as it choked on the blood. His lips were swollen and cracked, his eyes were puffy and closed over. Deep cuts scattered his face and freely leaked blood. Thalkin did not care, however. Instead, he turned back to Rosalind and knelt next to her. Although she was surely dead, Thalkin could not bring himself to pull out the blade. He looked down at her stomach and rested his hand there, crying freely.

There was a thundering of hooves and he heard a rider dismount. Thalkin did not have the energy for another fight. He simply turned around to see who it was. Edelia stomped through the bushes and stopped when she took the scene in.

'Thalkin...' Edelia wanted to ask what had happened, but realised he was in no state to talk now. 'We need to move, now.' Edelia marched over to Thalkin, looking around trying to take in as many clues as she could. She gripped Thalkin's arm and raised him to his feet. He tried to fight back and resist but he was weak.

'I cannot leave her,' he cried silently.

'Thalkin, you are bleeding.' Edelia saw the gash down his back and took a sharp intake of breath. It looked superficial but the loss of blood would be a worry. 'We need to move. There is nothing you can do for her.' She turned Thalkin to face her. 'Listen to me, I am not sure what has happened here, but it does not look good. We need to move now.'

'I did not hurt her, it was not me.' Thalkin's knees buckled again.

Edelia showed her strength when she gripped Thalkin by the tunic and half carried him out of the trees. 'I know you didn't Thalkin. I know, but no one else will believe you. Save a few.' They made it to the horses and Edelia's eyes were everywhere making sure they were not seen. The rain had softened slightly, and the sun had set. It was a cloudy night so they would have some cover from the moonlight while they rode off.

Just before Edelia helped Thalkin onto the horse she stopped and asked, 'Thalkin, did you do as you were told? Did you witness the meeting?' There were a few seconds and Thalkin sensed a rising tension.

He nodded. 'I have my notes in my bag, there is a lot to tell.' He felt like he needed to say this.

She slapped his shoulder and nodded for him to climb up. He winced as he was helped onto the back of the horse. 'We will treat your wounds when we get some distance, but we need to flee now.' Edelia hopped onto her horse and slapped the back of Thalkin's steed before kicking hers off. Thalkin gripped his reins tightly. Tears still brimmed his eyes, both from the pain of holding the reigns and the fatigue of the day, but also from what he was leaving behind. As the rain struck at his face, Thalkin felt a mixture of feelings. He was leaving Scor onto a new journey, a new life in which he would forge a life for himself and not be bound to his past. He felt the overwhelming pain and sudden loss of someone he had grown so close to. A void had been created in Sal's life, who did not even know how much his world had just changed. It was not the way Thalkin had imagined leaving Scor. Again, rage started to bubble. Ranic and Gregori had ruined the beginning of his new life and ended the life of Rosalind, one of the few people who had shown him kindness. Thalkin realised that he had the blade hovering over Gregori's throat, if only he had struck down with his blade, Rosalind would still be alive. Thalkin felt a deeper, hotter rage but worse still, it was directed at himself. He could have stopped what had just happened if only he had the courage. He promised himself he would never again hesitate to end someone's life to save someone he cared about.

Thalkin felt dizzy with all these thoughts and feelings but could do nothing but ride on and follow Edelia's horse. He would follow his teacher into the night no matter what dawn followed. Yet what made his head spin more than any thought or feeling was the suspicion that just before Edelia pulled him away from Rosalind, he felt a kick.

Made in the USA
Coppell, TX
06 May 2021

54762748R00095